D0445106

BROTHER *Just give them a chance to explain* SISTER

BROTHER / SISTER

Just give them a chance to explain

SEAN OLIN

raz**O**r
bill

An Imprint of Penguin Group (USA) Inc.

Brother/Sister

RAZORBILL

Published by the Penguin Group
Penguin Young Readers Group
345 Hudson Street, New York, New York 10014, U.S.A.
Penguin Group (USA) Inc., 375 Hudson Street, New York, New York 10014, U.S.A.
Penguin Group (Canada), 90 Eglinton Avenue East, Suite 700, Toronto, Ontario,
Canada M4P 2Y3 (a division of Pearson Penguin Canada Inc.)
Penguin Books Ltd, 80 Strand, London WC2R 0RL, England
Penguin Ireland, 25 St Stephen's Green, Dublin 2, Ireland
(a division of Penguin Books Ltd)
Penguin Group (Australia), 250 Camberwell Road, Camberwell, Victoria 3124,
Australia (a division of Pearson Australia Group Pty Ltd)
Penguin Books India Pvt Ltd, 11 Community Centre, Panchsheel Park,
New Delhi – 110 017, India
Penguin Group (NZ), 67 Apollo Drive, Mairangi Bay, Auckland 1311, New Zealand
(a division of Pearson New Zealand Ltd)
Penguin Books (South Africa) (Pty) Ltd, 24 Sturdee Avenue, Rosebank,
Johannesburg 2196, South Africa

Penguin Books Ltd, Registered Offices: 80 Strand, London WC2R 0RL, England

10 9 8 7 6 5 4 3 2 1

ISBN: 978-1-59514-386-0

Library of Congress Cataloging-in-Publication Data is available

Printed in the United States of America

WILL

How many times do I have to say it? Yes, I see the picture. You've been shoving it in my face for, like, the past forty-five minutes. And, yes, I understand what it is. It's a body, obviously. It's a dead body. I'm not blind, okay?

Sure.

It looks like it's been floating in the ocean for, oh, I don't know, a long time. Bloated, like it's going to split open that wetsuit it's been shoved into. And icy blue-white. I guess that's what happens when all the blood leaks out. The skin, it looks like a worm that you've been fishing with for too long, like spongy and pale and just gross. And, it's a guy. It's male. Maybe fifteen years old, I guess. Blond. Is he blond? It's hard to tell. I mean, first, it looks like the fish have been nibbling at him, and then also, his head's been smashed in, like with a baseball bat, or a golf club. His forehead, his eyes, his nose. There's basically just a crater where his face used to be.

No, this isn't easy for me. It sickens me. It's horrifying. It's not like I like looking at dead people. But—did you show this to Asheley? Tell me you didn't show this photo to Asheley. It would . . . She just . . . She doesn't need to see this. It would just be cruel. It would be too much for her.

Do I recognize the wetsuit? I don't know. I recognize the *type* of wetsuit. With those aerodynamic lime-green swoops up the sides of the legs. Yeah, it's a Quicksilver. But that particular one, how should I know if I've seen that particular one before?

I've already told you, maybe I do know who it is. Or maybe I don't. That depends. 'Cause there's a lot of assumptions you're making, I'm sure, and they're wrong. It was nothing like what you think it was.

Yeah, I'd love to explain. I'm eager to. I'll tell you everything.

For one thing. . . . No, first, I need to make one thing clear.

ASHELEY

You have to understand, I love my brother. I'm scared of him too, but . . .

That's why this is so hard. Regardless of what he has or hasn't done, I feel for him, you know?

Will's had a tough time. A whole lot tougher than I have. I was only four when our parents split up, and I can't really remember anything, but he was almost six. He understood what was going on and it was rough on him, totally disturbing. Mom actually sat him down after Dad left and said to him, "You're the man of the house now, Will. That's a lot of responsibility. If you can't handle it, who knows what might happen."

It must have terrified him. I know it did. To be six years old and told that if anything bad happens to your family, it'll be all your fault?

I don't know if she was drinking yet then. Probably. Maybe. Until this year, we never really talked about her drinking. It was just there. Crazy things would happen. She'd disappear for three days, and we'd get a call from the cops—excuse me, the police—way out in San Jose telling us to come pick her up. Or worse.

Will never figured out what to do with the emotions all this stirred up in him. By the time he was in middle school, he was getting in all kinds of stupid trouble—not criminal, not like he was turning into a delinquent, but he was volatile. Some kid would tease him about his new haircut, or like, pull the stupid yellow sweatband he always wore off his head, and he'd turn into a flurry of fists, spinning and flailing and not hitting anything, just himself, basically. It always made me sad. It was like something was exploding under his skin, like he was combusting. I remember once he brought a dead frog to school and kept it in his locker so long that you almost had to wear a gas mask to get past it. They had to evacuate the hallway and bring the fire department in to cart the thing away. It was like he was *trying* to repel everybody.

By the time he was a freshman in high school, he'd calmed down enough to not make a spectacle of himself all the time, but he still didn't have any friends. He'd sprouted up suddenly— he's six four—and he was crazy skinny because he hardly ever ate, just picked at whatever you put in front of him. He hung around in his bedroom, reading sports autobiographies and listening to, like, Interpol at full blast. The only time he ever left the house was to go out to the cliffs and drive golf balls as far as he could into the bay. In school he was like a ghost, hugging the walls so nobody would see him, sitting in the back of every classroom drawing pictures of these, like, skeletal people, these like malnourished ghouls playing basketball or tennis or golf or whatever. I think that's sort of how he saw himself.

It's not like it sounds. He has a good heart. You should have seen him when he jumped into action, when he had to bark Mom down from some drunken ledge. He could suddenly be more mature and capable than anybody the world's ever seen. It was just later that he'd shake for hours on his bed, sobbing. I couldn't console him no matter how hard I tried.

And things had just started to turn around for him this year. It helped that Mom had been on a bit of an upswing. She'd given up drinking. She was four months sober and she was cooking dinner for us sometimes and everything.

He trusted me. He always trusted me. And I always did the best I could to help him. I dragged him to CVS and proved to him that the cashiers weren't going to laugh at him for buying acne cream.

He was getting so, so, so, so much better. I'd finally convinced him that it was okay to take the sweatbands off and stop wearing that same striped polo shirt, tucked into his shorts, every day. I mean, he didn't suddenly turn himself into, like, a fashion icon, but at least he looked normal, at least he didn't seem so autistic anymore. And he was eating. He looked healthy. I caught him laughing at *Family Guy* sometimes. The girls were starting to whisper about how cute he looked.

And now ... I ...

I mean ...

I just, I wish there was some way to make sure he came through this okay.

So, as long as you keep that in mind while we do this, I guess, yeah, I can try to explain what happened and how we ended up down here in Mexico.

WILL

We're from Morro Bay. That's in California, like the foothills of Big Sur. Middle of nowhere California. It's not L.A., it's not San Francisco, it's not really anywhere. It's sort of tucked in there along the shore and hard to get to, so it's got a kind of snooty, closed-off air to it. There's a lot of money—like people who've made a fortune somewhere else move there to get away from the riff-raff. I mean, that's not true of everybody, it's still California, there's still people who've sort of bottomed out there, but even them, they're not anonymous. They're part of this sort of totally insular community. That's where our mom is.

I want to know that Asheley will be allowed to go back there.

She, maybe, won't be completely safe or happy, but at least she'll be somewhere familiar. She'll be able to think straight.

She'll, maybe, be able to figure out what comes next. I don't care what happens to me, really, I don't. But Asheley . . .

You have to believe me. She had nothing to do with any of this. It's not her fault. None of it.

Guarantee me that, and I'll tell you everything. Whatever you want to know.

Okay, then.

The guy in the photo. I know exactly who he is.

And yes. I killed him . . . but I had to. I had no choice.

Why? That's complicated. That'll take a while.

ASHELEY

The thing is that it had seemed like this summer was going to be better for us. Things had been looking up. Like I said, Mom had been sober for four months. And then . . .

Okay, I'm on the softball team and Will plays golf, and on this one particular Saturday in June, both of us had events. Mom hadn't managed to get to either one. Which was disappointing, but whatever. She might have been getting better with the alcohol, but she still had hard days. I'd figured she was hiding away at home so she wouldn't be tempted by the other parents drinking beer in the stands.

Will's event was a bigger deal than mine. He was at Hill Grove Country Club for the Countywide High School Invitational. It's like the championships for high school golf teams.

If you win, you get to play in the statewide competition at Hillcrest.

He'd texted me from the fifteenth hole: *I'm up four strokes! Maybe I'll win? WTF?!*

I was proud of him, relieved for him. Part of me was wishing I could be there to cheer him on.

And I was having a sort of breakout day too.

The Condors—that's our team, the Morro Bay Condors— were playing the Paso Robles Pumas that afternoon. They're a good team—our biggest rivals. For three years running, they'd gone neck and neck with the Condors right up to the end of the season, and we'd psyched ourselves up like crazy for this game.

This was my first year on the team and I was pretty mediocre. Freshman and sophomore years, I ran cross-country and it was just depressing. There's so much time to think when you're tromping down the side of the road all alone that you just inevitably end up going over all the ways your life totally sucks. This year, I decided to make a concerted effort. If Mom was changing her life, I figured, I should change mine too, or try to anyway, get out of the house, put myself in situations where I might make some friends. I was sick of doing things that isolated me, and I figured if I changed my attitude, joined a team sport, it would force me to get out of my head a little bit.

So far, though, I hadn't felt much camaraderie. I got along fine with the other girls, but we weren't exactly friends. I'm like that. It takes a lot for me to really trust anybody. I can be distant sometimes. I keep to myself a lot, sorting through the weird family things Will and I have had to deal with. When I'm around other people I put on a good face. I try to be chipper.

But that's not the same as actually allowing them to get to know me.

And I felt inferior, too, probably. Definitely. Sometimes I'd stand way out there waiting for a ball to come flying my way, sort of daydreaming and losing total track of the game and wondering why they put up with me at all. I mean, I'm not horrible. I've got coordination. I've got twenty-twenty vision, which helps me catch pretty well. But half the time, I can't hit. I can throw pretty well, but my aim's all off. I wouldn't know a balk if it hit me. No wonder they stuck me out in right field.

That day against the Pumas, though, since it meant so much, I tried extra hard to keep my head in the game. I kept track of the outs and made sure to set myself before every pitch, knees loose, glove hovering in front of me, ready to bolt in whichever direction the ball might be hit. When I was up at bat, I reminded myself to watch the pitcher's hand and follow the ball all the way to my strike zone. And then, when I swung, I reminded myself, push off on your back leg, that's where the power is, and swing with your whole arm—shoulder, elbow, wrist. It almost didn't matter if I made contact or not, what mattered was that I was completely ready, deep in concentration. Like they say, my head was in the game.

Good thing, too. The Pumas were fierce.

They had this girl on their team named Velasquez, a huge girl, her calves were like whole hams, and she could just crush the ball.

By the time I was up at bat in the fifth inning, they were beating us three to one, and that's with Becca throwing her eighty-six mile an hour fastball. Usually, nobody could hit those.

Talk about pressure.

We had runners on first and third and two outs. I was, of course, the number nine batter, which meant the Pumas, along with everyone else in the world, me included, figured I couldn't hit to save my life. Already in this game, I'd grounded a weak roller straight at the third baseman my first time up and struck out, like really struck out, completely whiffed the ball my second time up. The outfielders were playing in. And as I walked up to the plate, I could just sense the spirit leaking out of our dugout, like everybody already knew our rally was over.

I'd been in this situation before and what usually happened was that all the sounds around me thrummed louder and louder. I'd hear the catcher shuffling her knees in the dirt. I'd hear the ump coughing. I'd hear my teammates cheering me on. And the wind rustling the grass. When I tried to push these sounds out of my head, to concentrate like I should be doing, on the ball, they'd intensify. And then I'd have my own voice to contend with, the sound of my thoughts, saying, "Block it out. Feel yourself. Keep yourself loose. It's just you and the ball. Nothing else exists." And the things moving in my peripheral vision, stray napkins floating across the infield, the shortstop pounding her fist in her glove, everything. Until finally, all I could focus on was the tornado of distractions around me and the voice in my head screaming, "Stop thinking. Stop thinking. Stop listening to me!"

The thing is, this time, I wasn't nervous like I usually am.

It really was just me and the ball. It's hard to explain. It's like I was in a trance. I couldn't hear anything. The Pumas' pitcher kicked her leg up. Her arm started its pinwheel and the ball pushed forward. Time started moving really slowly. I could actually see the seams on the ball—I mean, who knew? I always thought that was a myth. I could see exactly how the ball was going to move, like I was peering up a track watching it roll toward me. There was a crack and a pain shot up my elbow and all of a sudden the sound came rushing back. Everybody was screaming. The chain-link fence around the dugout was rattling. "Run!" They were all shouting. "Run! Asheley, run!"

And oh did I ever run. Then I was aware of everything going on.

The ball floated over the left fielder's head, not because I'd hit it especially far, but because she'd been playing so far in that any fly ball would have gone over her head. I rounded first and made it safely to second by the time she'd gotten control and thrown it in.

Two RBIs! That was me who did that! It was exhilarating.

Naomi was up next. She, even more than Becca, was our all star. She's completely why the Condors have been so good the past few years. She could run. She could hit—not for power all the time, but she reliably put singles and doubles into the gap, which anybody who actually plays the game can tell you is actually better and harder to do. My God, could she field. Her position was shortstop, and I swear, nothing could get past her. At least once a game she made some leaping, contorting miracle play.

See, *she* had the right build for softball. The really good softball players are sort of boxy. They might be tall, but they've got bulked up shoulders and super muscular legs. That's Naomi—she was somehow able to be a total jock and still feminine and attractive to the boys. I think it's that she was curvy. All those muscles she had were softened by baby fat. She'd go to school in singlets and blood red shorts down to her knees (red's our school color, well, red and white—go Condors go!), and with her perfectly highlighted, perfectly buoyant hair, still manage to come off as glamorous.

And of course she hit me in. She got a home run. And I got to stand behind home plate and high-five her as she came around.

She wrapped her arm around my shoulder as we walked back to the dugout together. "Killer hit, Ash. You made her throw you the pitch you wanted."

For the rest of the game, she sat next to me on the bench, trash-talking the other team, comparing notes on which teachers I thought were the biggest pushovers and which ones scared the crap out of me, things like that.

It was weird.

And then, weirder, she said, "Hey, you're going to Becca's party, right?"

"Uh," I said, "I don't know. When is it again?"

"Wednesday. Don't tell me you're not going. Everybody's going. I'm sure Craig wants to go." Craig, my boyfriend. Well, my ex-boyfriend now, I guess. I'll get to him later. "Becca's parents bought something like five kegs. How can he resist?"

Becca's family owned a Spanish-style mansion tucked up in the hills north of town, a legendary place to the students of Redwood. They'd had the two or three acres of forest behind the house landscaped for some exorbitant amount of money. A swimming pool and hot tub carved right out of the rock. Lots of dark nooks and caves and places to disappear and smoke a joint or make out. For years, ever since her oldest brother had been a student, they'd been having end-of-the-year blowouts there. Her rich hippie-doo parents funded the whole thing and then always made sure to be away in Hawaii during the actual party itself.

"Maybe," I said. "I'll talk to him about it."

"Maybe? That's all I get?"

In my three years at Redwood, I'd never gone to one of Becca's parties. I'd thought about it the year before, but on the day of, I'd lost my nerve. I figured, if I was wanted, someone would have personally invited me, and now, here was Naomi doing exactly that.

"Okay," I said. "I'll be there."

"Promise?"

"Yeah."

She held her hand up between the two of us, her fingers curled into a loose fist. "Pinky promise?" We looped our pinkies around each other and pulled. "Oh, and you know what would be great is if you were able to drag Will along too."

"You want me to?"

"Sure." Naomi's gaze flicked away and back to me, like she was beating back a secret of some sort. "If you want, I mean," she said, almost too nonchalantly.

She liked him. Or anyway, she thought she might like him. That had to be it.

And this is, I guess, the point I'm trying to make. I could tell that day that my life was about to change. And what would that look like, you know what I mean? Because . . . it's hard to explain. He's never really had anyone he could talk to. And I know, the house can sometimes get too oppressive for him and he starts envisioning all the ways he'll be trapped in it forever, pushing and pulling at Mom and her addictions, forced to take care of her for the rest of her life. That's how he thought about these things.

I want to make sure I'm explaining this right. He's got crazy, overpowering protective impulses, and since he was little, he's believed there wasn't anybody out there—nobody but him— who cared enough to make sure Mom or me—I guess especially me—would be okay. I'm not saying that excuses him. I'm just... it just seems important to make that clear.

And, so on this day, when everything seemed to be full of hope for me, I wondered, how great would it be if Will could have something like that too? Like, if he could finally have some friends besides me? A girlfriend even! And one as cool as Naomi!

I was excited by the idea. And then, also, I was relieved by the thought that I wouldn't have to worry so much about him.

"Absolutely," I said to her. "I'm sure he'll be excited to go." Then, thinking, every little bit helps, I told her, "Hey, you know that tournament going on at Hill Grove? Will sent me a text a little bit ago. It looks like he might win."

She nodded her head, gazing off toward some intense place only she could see as she took this news in. "Cool," she said. "Very cool. You know what that means, right, Ash?" Cracking a half-smile, she scrutinized me waiting for the right answer. "Tequila shots! If you're going to celebrate, you've got to do it right."

By the end of the game, my imagination had gone wild on me. I couldn't help it. I kept imagining Naomi and Will and Craig and me racing around Morro Bay together all summer, kicking back at the beach all day, cool in our sunglasses, chasing each other around town as we drove from party to party on the weekends, being the glamorous kids everybody circled around on those nights when there was nothing to do but hang around in the woods, smoking pot and slamming beer, searching for the secret codes in the constellations. All these things I'd never done, all these ways Will and I were finally going to get to have the kind of normal high school fun that we'd always been too bunkered down to have before.

Really. This is what I was imagining. I guess I was naive, but what I really wanted, more than anything, was for us all to develop a kind of close-knit, kind of happy family feeling together.

And then we won the game, and as we did the loop of congratulatory high fives, the other girls on the team kept slapping my ass and saying things like, "Killer job, Asheley" and, "That was all you."

And you know? It was like a perfect day. Too perfect, maybe. I should have suspected that something would sneak up and clobber me.

There was even a sign. As we were packing the bats and helmets and stuff into the duffel bags, I saw Keith's rusty old green Eagle creeping up Verona toward Paradise Drive. I knew it was his because I recognized the giant Deadhead skull plastered across the rear window and the huge crack on the windshield. And he was going so slow, like ten miles per hour. I could tell he wasn't headed anywhere, just meandering around like he sometimes does.

Sorry. Keith is Mom's boyfriend. He's a little off. Smokes a lot of pot for "medicinal purposes." Sometimes he'll space out on you for what seems like hours—staring at you, his cheek twitching just a little. It's freaky. Mom claims it's PTSD, but come on, it was the eighties when he was in the army. He was stationed in Germany for, like, six months, but mostly he just sat around at Fort Hood.

One thing he's always reliable for, though, is letting me know when Mom's on a downswing. That's when he jumps in the Eagle and drives around town like a zombie.

Why didn't I wonder what was going on? Denial, maybe. Or maybe it was that, for one time in my life, I was being self-ish. . . . Either way, I regret it now.

WILL

Partly, it has to do with the fact that Mom got carted off to rehab again. I mean, she and I—when she's doing well, I'm doing well, and when she spirals down, I get, I don't know.

Bad.

I'm not making excuses. I'm not saying all of this is Mom's fault—it's my fault, I understand, it's all my fault—I'm just saying, there's a relationship there.

That was the day of the Countywide Invitational.

Yeah. I won. I shot a sixty-eight.

That was satisfying. It felt amazing, actually. Unbelievable. I'd never won anything before.

It was just like on TV. They laid out a big green carpet and propped me on a podium with the emblem of the Amateur

Golf Association of America plastered across the front of it and handed me a trophy.

That trophy. It was magnificent. Three feet tall, with a polished marble base and four long pillars ribbed in a metallic bluish material, and on top, of course, was the shiny statue of the golfer, his driver jacked up over his left shoulder and his head angled out toward the far edge of the fairway. It was heavier than I'd imagined it would be. Like something real. Something important.

While I was standing there, Red Gitney, the president of the company that was sponsoring the tournament, gave a speech about how important it is to support young athletes and all that boilerplate stuff and then we shook hands and people took pictures. There were journalists there. I was going to be in the papers and all the local websites. "How does it feel to be standing up there, Will?" one of them asked.

Not a hard question. Or it shouldn't have been, at least. But no way was I going to tell them the truth: that it felt totally surreal, like there'd been a mistake and I'd stepped into someone else's life, and it was freaking me out. I couldn't think of anything witty to say instead, though. I just stared out at the crowd and stuttered, trying not to faint.

Somebody finally shouted, "It's okay, kid, you said all you needed to say out on the links."

I think I smiled at this—I tried to. I didn't want to look ungrateful or anything.

Like I said, I was in a little bit of shock. The nervous shake in my leg was going crazy. I felt stupid, super self-conscious about the canary-yellow slacks I'd decided to wear that day.

Like I'd dressed myself up in a Halloween costume. And it was just dawning on me, now that I was standing there in front of everyone, that my shirt was three sizes too small. I kept swiping at my face thinking I was drooling or something.

I'm telling you, I was a mess.

Somehow, I got myself down off the podium though.

What I wanted was to find someplace to hide for five minutes, a secret room, someplace dark and cool and hard to find where I could breathe into a paper bag a few times, clear my head, try to at least remember my own name.

I headed up the pebbly white path that led to the clubhouse, nonchalant. Or trying to be, anyway. Reminding myself the whole way not to run.

People kept coming at me, though. Congratulating me. Grabbing at my hand and cranking down on my fingers. Pounding me on the back so hard you'd think they were trying to dislodge some chunk of food that had gotten caught in my windpipe. All these guys with pastel polo shirts tucked into their clown pants.

Every pro from every country club in like a hundred mile radius had shown up. They were old, like in their thirties, at least. And they had these wistful expressions on their faces—every single one of them, the same Yoda look—like they were remembering back to when they were the hotshot and wondering if they should encourage me to emulate their paltry lives or let me know now that it all ends in heartbreak, becoming a washed-up also-ran, adjusting the strokes of doctors and their ungrateful children.

And then there were the paunchy, even older guys with

their fifty-dollar haircuts and brightly colored ties. These were businessmen. They wanted to talk, to butter me up. Me! Like, who in their right mind would think I could be an important contact for them. They were talking about sponsorships, how if I gave a good showing in L.A., they were sure, I'd be hearing from Ping and Oakley and Adidas. One guy in particular, a sweaty, weedy guy with a salt-and-pepper crew cut who owned a coffee franchise I'd never heard of way up in San Francisco, kept nosing around about how I should attend Hunter Mahan's Teen Challenge Camp and asking if I'd thought about it, and if I could afford it and all sorts of questions like this. I figured out afterward that he was fumbling around trying to offer to pay, but by then it was too late, I'd blown him off in my desperation to get away from the crowd.

Finally, I was able to scramble inside. I ran to the bathroom and locked myself in a stall and sat there closed off behind those orange metal walls, staring in amazement at my new trophy. Imagining how great it was going to look when the nameplate had been affixed, and I had it sitting on top of the bookshelf in my bedroom.

That's when I was finally able to admit to myself this was real. I really had won.

I stayed in there for a long time. I could hear people shuffling in and out, flushing the urinals, turning the taps on and off. The blow-dryers. The clack of dress shoes on the tiles. That was fine though. I was isolated in my stall. I had room to think.

I'm not the kind of guy who wins things. I'm the guy bad

things happen to. The guy who, even when he's trying to do something nice, ends up making a big mess of everything.

Like, say, the time I tried to let Rose Lee bud in line in the lunch room because she wouldn't stop hissing at her friends about how they were running out of Rice Krispy Treats and she had to have one, it was the only thing that day that even looked edible. I said, "Rose, you can go in front of me if you want." And what did she do? She dropped her head down into her shoulders and gave me this revolted look like I was a sea creature, one of those giant squids they discovered a few years ago, and she was dumbfounded to learn I was capable of speech.

She turned to her friends. "Did he just speak to me?" There were three of them, Rose and her two friends, all of them clutching their flute cases to their chests a little tighter—as though I'd have any reason to try and yank them away.

"No, really," I said. "I'm letting you bud."

"No," she said, "That's okay." Then she went right back to complaining and whining about the Rice Krispy Treats and how she was going to "just kill myself if I don't get one."

Five more minutes of this and I tried again. I turned around. I half got out of line. I said, "Rose, really, just go in front of me. I don't care. I don't like Rice Krispy Treats." She pretended to not even hear me. "If you go in front of me, I'm sure you'll be far enough ahead in line to get one," I said. But no, she was too good to bother speaking to me. Rose Lee! With her plastic braces that are supposed be transparent but end up making it look like she hasn't brushed her teeth in ten years! I just lost it. "Or else shut the fuck up, Rose," I said. "Shut your fucking mouth about the Rice Krispy Treats if you're not going to let me help you get one." She was scared, I could tell. People were backing away from us. The line had disintegrated. It was all so stupid, but now that I'd started, I couldn't stop myself. "I could rip your throat out!" I said. "God damn it!" And when I couldn't think of anything more to say, I just opened my mouth and screamed as loud and long as I could.

That was me trying to do something nice. I got a week of detention for that one.

But look at me now.

I'd won! Me! Will Baird. Weird Willy Wanker. Even the guys on the golf team used to call me that.

This was some kind of vindication.

And locked in the bathroom stall, thinking about all this, I sort of broke down. I didn't cry. I was better than that. But I was scared for a moment there that I was going to, until there was a clatter and the stall suddenly started shaking and rattling and I was surrounded by the sound of my teammates' voices hooting and hollering in falsetto, trying to make themselves sound like little girls, saying things like, "Oh, Will, can I touch your trophy? Please? Pretty please? If I get it dirty, I promise I'll lick it off." And "How many strokes up are you now?"

"Yeah," I said. "It's me in here. You caught me. Leave me alone now so I can finish in peace?"

They quieted down for a second, then Lewis, who thinks he's hilarious, said, "Well, hurry the fuck up. You've been in there forever and we've got celebratory beer to imbibe." He used his real voice. This wasn't a joke. They wanted me to go binge drinking with them. That was new.

"I might be a while," I said. "Where you guys going?"

"Ricardo's house. His pop's out of town."

"Where's that?"

"Up on Gilmartin. The house with the totem pole out front."

"Okay. I'll meet you there."

The muscles in my shoulders and neck were tense. They didn't seem to be leaving.

"Hey, what did you do in there, Wanker? It smells like something died."

Then they slapped at the door again and raced off.

No way was I going to head up to Ricardo's. I didn't need their camaraderie. I didn't need their congratulations.

If I wanted that sort of thing, I would have joined the basketball team. It's the opposite of what makes golf so great. Golf is all about you and the elements. Other people have nothing to do with it. It's you and your weapons and your knowledge of physics and geometry and yourself. That's how I like it. And when I'm out there, choosing my clubs and planning my shots, lining up and taking my swings, I achieve a level of being in the world that transcends the complications and emotions and problems of my self. I'm me and I'm not me. I'm concentrating harder than ever, but at the same time, I'm not thinking at all. Thinking. Thinking and feeling. That's what's always getting me in trouble. When I'm golfing, there's none of that. When I'm shooting well, I enter a place where I'm in perfect balance with the world.

This was the real achievement of that day. Every single one of the eighteen holes I'd shot had burrowed me deeper into this perfect balanced place. If I was going to celebrate my win, the only way to do it was to find a way to stay in that place a little longer.

There's only one place in the world where I can achieve this feeling without a club in my hand, and once enough time had passed for me to be sure that the guys were long gone, I snuck away from the country club and headed there.

ASHELEY

The team was going to Shakey's, for pizza and unlimited salad bar. That's where they always went after a game. I usually skipped out, took off to hang out with Craig, even if that meant just watching him play Xbox.

Not today, though. No way.

I texted him. I was feeling playful. *Gotta bag. We won! Feeling startacular! Going to celebrate with the girls.*

Then it occurred to me, why not invite him along. If this was going to be my big coming out party, the beginning of the wild summer I'd envisioned, I should get things going on the right note, with everyone being crazy together. I shot him another text to say *Meet us at Shakey's. Free refills on Diet Coke!*

Shakey's is set up like a cafeteria, except it's a lot darker, with beer lights and hanging circular dome lights and framed pictures of sports stars on the walls. Instead of normal-sized benches and tables, it's got long shellacked wooden picnic tables, with twenty years' worth of graffiti gouged into them, and it's insanely popular, so if you go there with your family, you usually end up wedged in with four or five other groups.

The team is so big we took up an entire bench by ourselves, though.

When we arrived, there was a mad rush for seats, scrambling and elbowing, shouting and pointing. Everybody trying to make sure they got the spot they wanted next to the right people. Naomi did some juju to situate herself near the end of the bench and then she held the chair at the head of the table for me.

"Hey MVP," she said, "right here! The dad seat."

We ordered eight pizzas, and got some of them as half-and-halfs so the vegetarians wouldn't complain. Then, while we were waiting, we hit the salad bar. It's all you can eat, and that's the danger. When you can take as much as you want, how do you resist those extra four or five artichoke hearts or that extra half a pound of vanilla pudding? If you're not careful, you might put on fifteen pounds by the time you leave.

As we plowed into our salads and chugged at our massive forty-four-ounce cups of Diet Coke, Naomi ignored her usual crew. I could see, over her shoulder, the other girls playing musical chairs, zipping around to be closer to this or that more interesting conversation, but Naomi angled herself so that the two of us were cut off.

It felt almost like she was interrogating me, but in a nice way, more like she was checking off items on a list than like she was leading me toward incriminating myself. She kept asking me question after question about my life: what my summer job was going to be, if I had any pets, what my favorite TV show was. I told her: I'll be a scooper at Milky Moo's. No, no pets—Will's allergic. *The Daily Show*, absolutely, but I like *The Biggest Loser* too in a sick voyeuristic way.

"Besides Will and Craig," she asked, "who do you hang out with? I never see you around."

"Oh, I don't know," I said. "I'm sure you've heard—it's no secret, everybody knows—my mom's got some serious problems. She spends half her life down at Tuna Stewies, throwing back vodka tonics by the truckload."

Naomi didn't flinch as I told her this. Of course, it was true, everybody knew about my mother. She was the town drunk. There was no way to hide it. They'd seen her stumbling around by the docks and getting into fights with lamp posts. But still, Naomi held my gaze with her clear green eyes and listened like she really cared.

"I've only got so much time to deal with anything else besides her," I said. "And I guess, I'd rather have a few good friends who matter than run around crazy with a pack of people I don't really care about."

"How is she now?"

"She's been sober for four months. I think she might finally be moving toward okay."

"Wow!"

"Yeah, I can hardly believe it either."

Naomi looked up at the wooden crossbeams in the ceiling, really taking in how big a deal this was to me. We each grabbed a slice of the pizza that had finally come. Then she tapped my hand with her finger and said, "You're lucky. My family's not doing so great right now. They're getting divorced. It looks like it anyway." She went on to tell me about how her father was always traveling for work, conferences and things, and all the ways this had caused massive problems for her mother. Now her mom had started thinking he was having an affair. He wasn't— Naomi was pretty sure about that—but with all the accusations and arguments this was causing, things were getting pretty horrible pretty much all the time.

Until that day, Naomi had never said more than two words to me. She'd never been unfriendly. I'd just figured I didn't rank. I'd never been shiny or sparkly or interesting enough for her to bother trying to get to know me—her friends had always seemed so obsessed with status, with success. They were constantly building up their extracurriculars and padding their applications to Stanford and Yale and Columbia and striver schools like that. I mean, Naomi had a freak God-given talent, but the rest of them were just Joiners. That's what Will and I called them behind their back. The Joiners.

It was a nice shock to the system to realize that Naomi had some depth to her, too.

And I was excited, flattered, that she'd opened up to me like this.

"So, but, you're definitely coming to the party, right?" she said, changing the subject.

"It's a deal," I said.

"Good. Pinky swear!" We did the pinky flick thing again.

Then she fished an ice cube out of her glass and leapt up on her knees to throw it at Becca.

"You did not just do that!" Becca said. She threw a cube back.

And Naomi threw two more, one a direct hit and the other whizzing off to land smack in the middle of Ruth's mushroom slice. This started a war. Ice was flying everywhere, everyone shrieking and shouting and cackling. I even worked up the courage to throw a few cubes of my own. It was all very silly, just stupid fun.

But thrilling.

Then all of a sudden, someone clamped their hands tight over my eyes. A boy, I could tell from the rough feel of his skin. Craig. Of course. Who else could it have been? He'd finally made it. And you have to believe me, I was glad he'd come.

"Guess who?" he said. He was using his frog voice, sort of belching the words out.

I let my head fall back into his abs. Craig was really strong, even if, with his lanky surfer build, he didn't look it. I reached around and felt up his calf muscles.

"Craig?"

"No, I'm not Craig," he croaked.

Sometimes Craig liked to be goofy like this. I started listing off the names of his surfing buddies.

"Uh, Angel?"

"No."

"Pauly?"

"No."

"Tracer?"

"No."

"Alex?"

His hand shot up off my eye for a second and he said, in his normal voice, "Hey! Don't throw ice at me!" Then he clamped it back down and went back to the frog voice. "Guess!"

I'd run out of surfer dudes to rattle off, so I said, "Will?"

"Fuck no. It's me, Ash," he said, pulling his hands away and tipping my head back for an upside-down kiss. He'd been drinking. It was all over his breath. And in the slightly pushier, rougher way he was handling me. Annoying.

"Then why'd you say no when I guessed your name?"

"I was fucking with you, babe," he said.

Still, I was glad he'd come. Craig was a much more social person than me. He could be a real party boy when he wanted to. When he wasn't sunk in one of his moody swings, holed up in the dark playing video games, or out on the waves by himself in the dark.

I scooched over in my chair to make room for him next to me. He put an arm around my shoulder. Then he took it away again and picked up the slice of sausage and onion I'd been nibbling at, folded it in half, and took a humungous bite.

His buddies were all with him. They circled the table, high-fiving the girls and stealing food along the way, until they found places to squeeze in and join the party.

And everything seemed to be fine for a while. There were more ice wars.

One of Craig's friends, Pauly, had run into the guys on the golf team at the Exxon station that everybody bought their beer at because it never carded. Turned out Will had won. I was glad for him.

"Was he with them?" I asked. "Was he celebrating?"

I wanted him to be having the same revelatory kind of day I was.

"Naw. I didn't see him," Pauly said. "Anyway, those guys are tools. I can't imagine even Will wanting to hang with them."

For a second, I wondered why he hadn't been in touch to tell me the news himself. I wondered if he was maybe not okay. But I didn't wonder very hard. Not as hard as I should have.

"Hey," Naomi said, "you should call and congratulate him."

I must have known he wasn't okay, actually. Otherwise I wouldn't have protested like I did. "I'll text him instead," I said, whipping out my phone.

"And say congrats for me, too," Naomi said.

While I typed in the message, Craig slid his arm under the table and started tickling all over my knee, running his finger up the inside of my thigh. I leaned into him a little, pressed my knee up against his to let him know I was glad he was here.

As soon as I was done texting, I reached down and held his hand and he slipped his fingers out of mine and started trying to play handsy with me, flicking his fingertips across my palm, lacing and unlacing them with mine, tickling, like halfway between finger dancing and groping. It made me twirl a little inside, to have Craig so conspicuously wanting me in front of everybody, but still.

"Stop it!" I mouthed.

"Stop what?" he said, looking around like, *gee whiz, who me?* And at the same time, he slid his hand off mine and started running his finger up my inner thigh again. He wasn't doing it in an aggressive way, or he wasn't trying to, but he was drunk and we were right there in front of everybody. It didn't feel as good as I'm sure he'd hoped it would. I grabbed his hand and pulled it back to my knee.

"That! And shh! Everybody can hear you."

"Ash. Asheley, Ash," he said. "I can't help myself. You're looking so hot in that uniform."

"No I'm not. And even so—" I tilted my head toward everybody around the table. They'd noticed, a few of them had anyway. Even if they were pretending not to, I could tell they were keeping track of us out of the corner of their eyes.

"You are, Ash. Polyester pinstripes. They make me crazy."

Our jerseys are the kind that button up the front, and right there at the table with the whole team and all his surfer buddies as witnesses, he started fumbling with the top button.

"Stop it, Craig. I mean it. Not here."

"Then let's go someplace else. Tracer's Tahoe is right out back. Let's climb in the back window and go for a ride. Get it?"

"Yeah. I get it." I was starting to get fed up with him. It was like he was not taking the hint on purpose.

He'd never been like this before. I mean, he'd been frisky, sure, but usually he at least noticed a little bit whether I was feeling the same vibe as him.

"Are you crazy, Craig? How much did you guys drink before you got here? I'm with the team. I'm having fun. Can't you see that? Have you ever seen me go out with the team before?" I was hissing at him now.

Naomi had inched down the bench. She was pretending to

be part of the conversation Colleen and Amy were having, but she wasn't saying anything and her head was angled perfectly to catch every little thing that happened with me.

"Don't be like that," Craig said. He let go of me. He folded his hands in his lap and sat there, staring at the names gouged into the table.

For a few minutes, we both sat there in silence. I watched Naomi watching Colleen and Amy and ran through things I might say to instigate a new conversation with her, but I couldn't come up with anything to say. All I could think of was Craig sulking next to me like a slug, sucking all the happiness out of my evening.

Finally I turned to him. "What? You're just going to pout now."

"No."

"Then what would you call what you're doing right now?"

He cracked half a smile and threw me a mischievous look. "How about a kiss. Just one. With some tongue action?"

That was it. I couldn't take any more. I leapt up and grabbed him by the hand and pulled him outside.

He camped it up, waving at everybody, doing the call me thing to his friends with his fingers like it was all a big joke, but he came with me. He didn't resist.

I should say, Craig wasn't always such an asshole like this. He really wasn't. He was usually a pretty great guy.

He liked to pretend he was a kind of carefree lost boy, rolling like the waves across the ocean of his life, too zen to bother asking what it all meant. But that's just the image he wanted people to see. Him with his shirt off, showing off his Polynesian shoulder tattoo, his bright patterned surfer shorts riding so low that you could see a wisp of blond hair floating over the laces. He was usually the kind of guy who would laugh along as the day took him wherever it went. Laughing and laughing at everything—sometimes, sure, in a cruel macho way when he was with his dudes, but not always. When he was with me, we'd laugh together at the crazy things my mother put me through—or his dad, his dad had put him through some kind of hell. It was like enough laughing would solve everything in the world.

I loved that about him. Together, we made each other feel better, no matter how horrible things might be. And anyway, if I wanted a serious conversation, I had Will for that.

That night, though, maybe because it seemed like I was auditioning for a bigger, better life for myself, I wasn't seeing the humor in his games. I feel bad about that now. I feel like . . . maybe if I'd been less hard on him, then . . . I don't know. Forget it. That's a stupid thought.

I marched him around the corner of Shakey's red brick facade so nobody would spy on us through the front windows, and then, arms folded across my chest so he'd know not to mess with me, I said, "Can we be done with this, now? I'm completely serious."

"Done with what? I thought you were bringing me out here so I could feel up your boobies. Are you dumping me, now? Why? Because I can't help being attracted to you? You'd rather have a boyfriend who thinks you're ugly?"

God. I almost burst into tears right then and there.

I was able to sputter out, "I'm not dumping you."

"So . . ." He sashayed up and wrapped his arms around me, pulling me toward his groin.

"I'm not dumping you, Craig," I said again. "I'm just . . . They like me. The team. I did good today and now they want to be my friends. Can't . . . I mean . . ."

I was completely breaking down, pounding my fists on his chest. The tears were rolling down my cheeks. Why did I have to spell everything out for him? It was so obvious. Didn't he know anything? Couldn't he see how important this was to me?

"Right. I get it, Ash. That's why we're celebrating," he said. "So, come on, celebrate with me."

I guess not. He didn't get it at all. He was going to keep wheedling and rationalizing with me until I wore down and gave him what he wanted.

"Can we do that later? Please? Can I just have fun with my new friends first? Then we can go back to your house and whatever. Okay? Please? Just like another half hour?"

"Hmm." He drummed his lip. "Okay, but how about a kiss to seal the deal?"

At that point, I didn't have much of a choice. We kissed. A soft lippy kiss that I cut short as soon as he started to try probing with his tongue.

He raised his fists in the air and shouted "Victory!" real slow like Kevin Dillon's always doing on *Entourage*. And we headed back inside.

When we got to the door, I realized I couldn't let everybody see me, not like this. I had to at least get myself together first. I hung back and let him go in without me.

The whole table turned to look when he walked in. I was watching through the window. When he noticed he had their total attention, he did the "Victory" pose again and then shimmied around in this cornball knock-kneed dance. Like nothing had happened. Being goofy, fun Craig again.

I could just imagine what they were all thinking. But it's not like I could do anything about it. They were going to think what they were going to think no matter what I told them had happened outside. No way could I go back in there and take my walk of shame. Not if it meant seeing Naomi and the other girls on the team laughing at me. Not today. This was supposed to be the day when things changed. For the better, I mean.

It was all too much for me.

I fled.

I jumped in my car and headed home. I feel horrible about that. Part of me—a big, aching part of me—wonders how things would have gone differently if I'd had the courage to stick around, to, you know, tough it out. Then maybe Craig and I could have talked through the problem and . . . I don't know. Things could have gone differently.

WILL

The one thing we've still got from back when Dad was around is our house. Everything else might be worn out and falling apart, second-rate, on the verge of being repossessed due to the mess Mom's made of all of our lives, but the house keeps getting paid for. Dad sends a check every month.

It's an amazing house. Dad's an architect—or he used to be, who the hell knows what he's up to now—and he designed it himself. Sort of a modern rustic vibe. Dark wood, exposed beams, lots of open spaces, sky lights and big windows. It's set up so that each room almost has a floor to itself, like tiers, each one connected to the others by a couple wide steps and a series of platforms, spiraling around this huge, cavernous living room. It's hidden away behind an acre of forest and the backyard's huge too. This sort of hilly sprawl. Behind that, there's more forest, redwoods and cedars, a prickly carpet of pine needles, like two inches thick, everywhere. And then the cliffs, which are hard to get to right behind the house, but if you follow the trail maybe half a mile south, you end up at an opening where you can sit right on the edge and look out at the bay.

That's where I went after I left the country club. I didn't even bother to drive all the way home, just parked along the side of the road and took the short cut where Paradise bends closer to the bay.

It's my favorite place in the world. There's a boulder there that's, I swear, shaped like a rabbit. I like to climb up and huddle in under the ears, and just watch what happens. You'd think you were on the edge of the earth, a thousand miles from anything. There's eagles sometimes, and hawks, and if you follow them long enough, you can see them dive bomb for fish.

I don't know. It just makes me feel right, being there. Whatever's going on, I get to that cliff, and I remember who I am. I can think straight up there.

That day, the sun was just setting when I got there. You get an unbelievable view from the cliffs: the shadows creep out, and different colors streak across the water—dark purples and yellows and reds.

My head was still spinning from the weirdness of how everybody'd been treating me. Here on the cliffs, all of that fell away. It was just me and the world—and my trophy. I studied it. Every inch. I placed it in various spots on the cliff and looked at how it changed depending on the background. Facing the bay, I held it with two hands high above my head, just like I'd done on the podium, and shouted, "I did it! Vindication! You happy with me now?"

Who was I shouting to? I don't know. The birds. The rocks. The mountains. The ocean. For a second there I thought my dad might even hear, though how could he? He lives way down here in Mexico.

Then, having made my peace with the wilderness, I wandered back to my car and drove the final little stretch of road home.

I should have known as soon as I got there that Mom had gone all to hell again. The signs were obvious, once I figured it out. All the lights were on. There was a carton of orange juice out on the counter, not even screwed closed. The Guns N' Roses— it's always Guns N' Roses—was blasting out of the speakers in the open living room area, filling the whole house. The door to her room, up there at the top of the platforms curving around the main part of the house, was closed. I was stupid though. Thinking she was fine. Thinking there was no way she'd fall down again.

First thing I did was I turned down the music. Then I called up to her, "Hey, Mom, check it out. You'll never guess what I did."

Then I waited.

It took her, like, five minutes, maybe longer, to open her door. She leaned out over the railing, frowning at me way down in the living room. "The music, Will. I was listening to that," she said.

I had to crane my neck to talk to her up there. She was wearing that red-and-brown Tibetan knit cap she likes so much. It's like her security blanket or something. "Can you come down here a second?" I said.

"Why?"

"I've got something to show you."

"What?"

"Just . . . a thing, Mom. It's important." I don't know why I was hiding the trophy like this. I had this image in my head of her sitting on the big white couch in the living room and me displaying it on the coffee table, like placing it on its throne and seeing her ooh and ah.

"Well, bring it up here, then."

"Mom, please."

I sat down on the swivley white leather footrest that floats around the living room, and propped my trophy on the table.

"What's that?" she called.

"It's the thing I want to show you."

"Okay, I'm coming down, but only because you turned down my music."

Mom started making her way slowly down the platforms curving around the room. Her hand never left the railing, clutched it so tightly her knuckles turned white. After each step down, she stopped for a second, recalibrating her balance, fake smiling at me.

That's when I finally realized she was bombed.

I picked at a fleck of dirt that had gotten stuck to the figurine, feeling suddenly like someone had kicked my knees out from under me. I wasn't special anymore. How could I have ever thought that?

By the time she got to the bottom, I'd decided, why bother.

She came and stood right behind me, not getting too close, but hovering there. I could feel her heat behind me, studying my trophy, feeling sheepish and remorseful, I was sure, trying to come up with the right thing to say. Then she swiped her hand at my head, playfully, like she was flirting with me. Of course, she missed.

"Did you steal that?" she said. That's her idea of a joke.

I refused to answer her.

She wandered around the table and sat on the couch.

"You won," she said.

"I won."

She was beaming. Just . . . so proud of me. Shocking. I mean, really. This wasn't the kind of situation I was used to with her, this being pleased with me. This noticing me.

She was crying she was so happy. I could almost see the beautiful, natural woman she'd been back in the days before Dad had left, shining through. The dimpled cheeks. The capacity for awe.

And then we were both crying. Like chumps. Like sentimental fools. I didn't even care that she was drunk all of a sudden. All that mattered was that she was proud of me. She lifted the trophy off the table and held it in her lap, running her finger along the outline of the golfer on top, cradling it, like it was hers, a baby she'd protect with her life if she had to.

"I knew you'd win," she said. "I had a feeling this morning. Like a vision of you all dressed in white and glowing with an overpowering, blinding light. And I just knew. You'd outgrown the sensitive boy you used to be and now you were going to show the world the man you'd become." She stopped then. She stared at the trophy, moving her lips but not saying anything. She was working something out in her head. "I liked that sensitive boy," she said.

"I'm still me, Mom."

"You're still you." She got quiet again.

There was a time, when I was young, before Dad left, and for a little while after that, when I'd thought my mom was the most amazing person on earth. She just . . . she'd seemed so strong, holding us together as a family, regardless of what horrible selfish thing Dad had done this time. She'd talk to me like I was a little adult. I mean, like I was her friend, her partner in survival, and I just happened to be a short little guy. She'd hold me on her lap and sing me these songs that she made up off the top of her head about how special and noble and brave I was. And I believed her. I remember, I felt like we were in the fight together, like she would help me and I would help her, and if we just kept at it, we'd find a way to pull ourselves—and Asheley, of course, all of us, the whole family—we'd pull ourselves up out of the junk heap that was our lives and we'd, like, soar away. We'd leave it all behind.

That was back when she had her drinking under control. I mean, I don't know. She was . . . She'd been . . . pristine, at least to me. Full of hope and passion. And maybe this was stupid of me, but I'd thought after her last stint in rehab that the other person inside her, the one, the, like, brilliant, golden warrior she had inside her would come galloping back. I'd thought the broken-down person she'd become was going to be gone forever.

But no.

When she's drunk, her emotions are like physical forces that tug and pull at her body, beating each other up inside her. And this day, when I got home from the invitational, something was going on now in there. She was trying to control it, but there was ugliness yanking at the edges of her mouth.

"Too bad you can't tell your dad about this," she said. "He'd cream himself. Golf was the most important thing in the world to him. Or that was the story, right? He'd stand on that cliff out there and send balls out into the bay for four, five hours at a stretch. He cared more about golf than he did about me."

"Mom, don't." I knew how this went. She got on the topic of Dad and it could only end two ways—either she was wailing for the rest of the night about how terribly she missed him, how perfect and caring and tender he was, or she was screaming about that asshole who ruined her life, so smug and selfish that she could have disappeared into the ocean and it would have been weeks before he noticed she was gone. "Don't ruin this."

"Don't ruin this. Don't ruin this." She turned the words over in her mouth like they were made of sand. "It's always me ruining things. Right, Will? Is that it?"

"Mom."

"You men have it all figured out. Everything has its little place and as long as I stay inside mine and smile and pat you on the head it's okay, but guess what, Will, you're the child and I'm the mother, and you don't get to decide what I can and can't say."

"Mom, you're not making sense."

"Your ass, I'm not. Don't ruin this. Bah." She spit. She actually spit. Not at me, but she sent a big gob across the table. "I

know what 'don't ruin this' means. It means don't go snoop-
ing around learning about things you don't want to know. It
means I can fuck any old *intern at my firm* I want and your job is
to have the kids off at school by seven and dinner on the table
and don't ask questions. Is that how it is, Will? Now that you're
a big man champion golfer? You're going to make sure you
keep me in my place?"

"Forget it," I said. I almost wished I'd lost the stupid golf
tournament.

"Don't tell me to forget it. I'm the parent here."

Sometimes the only thing to do is beg her to stop. To plead
with her. That's what I did now. "Everything's okay, Mom. I
was just trying to show you the trophy I won. It's not important. I'm tired. I'm going to go to my room now."

When I tried to take it from her, she pulled it tighter to her
chest and twisted around to avoid me.

"Sure. Go. Storm off. Isn't that typical. You're just like—"

And I totally lost it. "Don't you dare! Don't you ever! I am
not. I'll never be like that man. If you weren't such a drunk,
maybe you'd—" I was screaming at the top of my lungs. Just,
total blind rage.

And then she leapt up and took a swing at me. With my trophy. I tried to get out of the way, but she caught me in the arm.
The golfer on top of it—you know, it was posed in mid-swing,
the club sort of jutted up away from its body—and this club
sort of hooked my skin and sliced. It was pretty deep. Blood. It
stung. All that.

See? Right there. I've still got the scar.

She came at me again and I ducked and sort of fell back and

went sprawling onto the floor and my trophy whizzed past like a baseball bat and Mom went spinning after it, losing her balance and tripping over herself and falling into the coffee table. Like, really falling. She hurt her wrist really badly where she'd tried to catch herself, and she sort of tumbled over and pulled herself up onto the couch, whimpering and crying and holding her hurt hand and staring at it. And I saw later, she'd cracked the glass a little bit in the corner of the table.

The horrible thing was that in that moment I didn't even ask myself if she was okay. I was worried about the trophy. If she'd broken it or something.

I crawled across the floor and pulled it toward me, and right away, I saw that the golfer had snapped off.

My body felt like it was made out of concrete. Like my evil emotions were pulling me through the floor. I was turning into mud. I sat there where I'd fallen and just . . . I don't know, I was paralyzed.

ASHELEY

The phone?

Drop dead?

I mean, yeah, I guess I did send him a text saying that, but, I mean, there was a reason. It wasn't just . . .

Well, if you've got his phone, then you can see for yourself. There's a context for all those text messages I sent him.

So, okay, so, here's where it starts, right? I couldn't have been more than three blocks from Shakey's when I got the first text from Craig asking where I'd run off to.

Home. I couldn't take it. I wrote back.

Ten seconds later I got his response. *Couldn't take what?*

Everything.

And what did he say to that? How did he respond to my

telling him I was totally emotionally overwhelmed? He said, *What about our deal?*

And you have to imagine how misunderstood I felt when I saw that. I was getting more and more upset.

The light I'd been stopped at turned green, and I don't like to text while I'm driving, so I dropped my phone in my lap. Craig can wait, I figured. I'd get back to him at the stop sign up the road. By the time I got there, he'd shot off three more messages.

What about our deal?!!

Were you lying?

Write me back! Fucking A!!

This was going to take a while. I pulled onto the gravel along the side of the road and put my car in park.

I wrote him back. *Sorry. Driving. :)*

And he wrote: *How bout I come over?*

No.

So you lied to me?

You're drunk. I'm tired. Talk tomorrow?

Not too drunk to fuck.

Real Mature, Craig.

Immature's better than frigid.

Keep it up, Craig. That's the way to change my mind.

I couldn't help wondering what kind of spectacle he was making of himself back at the restaurant. I could just see him narrating our text war for the crowd, reading my messages and making sarcastic comments about them, trying to get everybody to laugh at my behavior, getting them to group-think what to write back.

Since you won't put out, maybe I should call one of my other bitches.

If his goal was to make me paranoid, it worked. Everybody liked Craig, even if they didn't take him all that seriously. He was the kind of guy you wanted at your party. He upped the goofiness factor. I was sure there were other girls out there who'd love the chance to try to tame him. But I was too pissed at him to go begging for explanations.

I typed back: *Is that a threat or a promise?*

Both. I'll make sure to send you the photos.

Why did I put up with him? Good question. I have no idea. No. That's not true. I put up with him because when he wasn't acting crazy like this, he was crazy in love with me, and there aren't that many guys out there who care enough to try and make you feel special. But at that point, I'd had about all I could take. If this was how special felt, he could have it back.

And yeah, in the last message I sent him, I said, *Drop dead, Craig!!* But, I mean, it wasn't a threat. I was just trying to make sure he understood how totally pissed I was at him.

Then I turned my phone off. Let him be the one to suffer for a while. I sat there in the dark along the side of the road for, I don't know, half an hour, listening to my iPod and trying to talk myself down from hyperventilating.

I was overwhelmed, you know? Not really thinking about what I was saying. You can't really think I meant I wanted him dead. I swear, I didn't. He was my boyfriend! I loved him!

WILL

That's when Skeezy Keith showed up.

Or, not exactly. He'd been there for a while, hovering in the dark outside the glass doors, hidden by the reflections, watching us go at it. He's always doing this. He's a total lurker, tugging at the bottom of his flannel shirt, his big bug eyes bulging into his giant plastic glasses like they're trying to pop out and run across the room. But that's when he decided to stop creeping around and do something to help.

He slid open the door and wandered onto the little step-thing that leads down into the room. "Hey," he said. And he threw his hand up above his head and gave a kind of loose wave. "Maybe it's time for us all to chill out a little, huh?" No matter how tense the situation, no matter how crazy and out of control, Keith talks like he's some sort of half-wit cowpoke, slow as ice, like he's messing through the information coming at him and gradually, gradually, putting it together into an intelligent thought. Too many drugs. That's what you get.

Mom gave him a look, like, you want a piece of this too? And then she let loose this tirade. "Oh, look at the big man coming to save the day? Is that it, Keith? You think you're gonna protect him?" And then she, like, hissed at him—actually hissed! Like a cat! She was spraying spit everywhere while she talked. "Try me. I'm just getting started."

Keith just stood there, staring, like he'd taken a handful of Valium or something. That's his way. He thinks somehow that if he stays completely passive, she'll realize how crazy she's acting and give up. Which never happens. It just spurs her to get more hopped up and spiral completely out of control.

"What's it to you, anyway? You're not his father. Ha. If only. What a laugh that would be."

Nothing from Keith. Just more of that staring. He dug his fists into his jeans pockets and waited.

"Good thing it could never happen, huh?"

She was so focused on Keith now that I'd been forgotten and part of me thought I should make my escape, crawl out of the room and flee back to the cliffs, where the hard stone and wilderness were more predictable and I might be able to sink back into myself.

"Huh, Keith?" she said.

I don't know what kept me there, honestly. I kept thinking about my trophy. Staring. Fixated. Wishing there was some way I could snatch up the pieces and pull them to me and press them back together and make them whole.

"Good thing. You're broken down there. Didn't know that, Will, did you? Good thing, too. Imagine, little Keiths running around? Leering at all the little girls they can't have?"

By now Keith had slipped down to sit on the step. Holding his phone like a threat between his legs. That same defeated look plastered across his face.

"Right, Keith? Right? Say something, you asshole!"

She kept at him like this, pulling herself up from the couch sometimes to shove her finger at him and stomp her foot, then tumbling back, falling over herself. She must have drunk a gallon of vodka at least before I got home. The alcohol was metabolizing in her system now. She was getting so bombed she could barely hold herself upright. And wherever she landed, she'd swear at Keith, and me too, if she noticed me, like it was all our fault.

Then she started throwing things. Scraps of paper that she crunched into balls, pens, PS3 game cartridges, anything she could find. There was a hammer—Keith must have been working on something that day. He makes his living as a carpenter, pick-up jobs. Works with a few contractors around the area. And when he's not working, he sometimes putzes around our house fixing things. He's always leaving his tools all over the place. Anyway, when she cranked that at him, it flew into the wall and left a massive gouge.

That's when he called the Christers. He didn't say anything, just flipped open his phone and punched in the number.

The Christers is just what Ash and I call them. Their real name is Family Life Blood Church. They're a kind of crunchy gooey group of Jesus fanatics. And they run a weird, sort of cultish rehab center called Hope Hill, where Keith got sober a few years ago and where Mom had gone a bunch of times, too, but, obviously, without the same results. Keith was, well, I'm not sure if he was a believer or what. I guess he was. It's not like he went in for all their weird rules or anything, and he didn't talk about it with us much. He knew Asheley and I thought it was a bunch of bullshit. But he did, like, visits to shut-ins with them, though, and he always let them use his Eagle to cart stuff back and forth to the beach for the weird loaves-and-fishes thing they did every Easter.

It took me a second to realize this was what he was doing. Not until he was talking to them, laying down the address, saying, "Yeah, she really needs some help." The Christers know our place. We've been through this before. It always ends tragic.

"No!" I shouted. "Fucking Keith, no!"

I leapt up and threw myself at him, trying to wrestle the phone away from him, but no matter how skinny and out of it Keith looks, he *was* in the army. And in juvie before that for stealing some bozo's Camero back in the day. He knows how to fight. He's fast. And stronger than you think. He pushed me back and I came at him again and got my arms around his waist and we started wrestling each other to the ground, throwing fists when we could. Kicking and flailing and knocking into everything. I don't know what I was trying to achieve. Mom was cackling at us, like this was the show she'd been waiting for all this time.

And then the big white van the Christers drive around showed up and that was that.

ASHELEY

Yeah, I caught the tail end of that thing with Mom.

It was close to ten by the time I made it home and when I got there the first thing I saw was the white van stalling there in the driveway, its back doors flung open, and I knew right away what had happened. The Christers were here. Oh, crap.

Don't get me wrong. I don't have anything against Jesus, or God, or whatever. I sort of sometimes think I even believe in him, but the Christers, they were something else entirely. I mean, it was like, besides believing in God, they wanted to "walk in Jesus's footsteps," which meant, basically, they tried to live like people in Biblical times. The sandals. The togas. The berries and nuts. It's not like they shoved this stuff down anybody's throat, but still. Weird, you know? They were Keith's friends.

And if they were here, that meant something crazy must have happened. Mom was dragged out of the house before I even made it out of the car. Two bearded guys, one on each arm, and her bucking and skidding, her face red and blotchy, her hair flying wild, stumbling and lurching as the guys coaxed her down the driveway.

Just what I needed. A great capper to a great day, right? Something good had happened to me, and duh, of course, that means everything's got to turn into total crap. But what could I do? I got out of the car and headed toward the house trying to make like this was all normal everyday stuff—which, I guess, it sort of was. I'd just been stupid enough to get my hopes up, to think over the past few months that it might be possible for things to turn out okay for her. Us. Whatever.

She saw me, of course. We walked right past each other. I wasn't sure if I should try to hug her or what, but it didn't matter, because she got this ugly look on her face and started jumping around and pulling away from the guys. They were holding her elbows so tightly that their fingers were turning white, whispering to her in that way they did.

She squawked at me, "Ash! Ash!"

I said, "Hi Mom." Totally defeated. Just, too much of everything.

"Don't go in there," she said. "Your brother's in there."

"Yeah," I said. "Okay."

"He's . . . You tell him . . . I'll be paying attention. If he touches you—if he does anything to hurt you—he has no idea, I'll . . ."

Before I could think, she was being shoved into the back-seat of the car and the door was slamming on her.

And one of the guys taking her to the van, just a little guy, but stocky—he looked like he was barely older than me—gave me a kind of weirdly blissful half-smile, like he somehow thought I'd appreciate the great kindness he was doing for her. I almost told him to go fuck himself, but I caught myself. That would have just made it worse.

As I went inside, I ran smack into Keith. His greasy backpack was thrown over one shoulder, and he seemed a little twitchy, but, given what was going on, he was calmer than you'd think. He was taking the Eagle, he said, to follow behind the Christers and deal with the paperwork and whatever else, keep an eye on her.

"Okay," I said. I didn't really care. Or I cared about her, in a complicated, infuriated way, but I couldn't have cared less about what he was up to. What I wanted was for him to let me get past him so I could find Will and see if he was okay. I figured he wasn't. I mean, obviously. No wonder he hadn't responded to my texts.

But Keith lingered. In that creepy way of his. He sort of held himself back like he wanted to touch me, to pat my shoulder, or give me a hug or something, to comfort me, but then also thought maybe that was inappropriate, like he didn't trust himself to be touching me no matter how harmless those touches might be.

"Okay," I said. "Bye. You better get going if you're going to catch them." And I backed along the wall to get around him.

I called out for Will, but he didn't answer, so I went sleuthing through the open chambers on the ground floor level of the house. I found him in the living room area, balled up like a potato bug in the corner behind the stereo. Like he'd found the smallest, most hidden spot in the room to tuck himself into.

"Will?" I said. "You okay? What happened?"

He didn't answer. He barely even bothered to look up.

Except for all the shattered people around me, it didn't look like there'd been that huge a scene, not by our standards, at least. There weren't any gaping holes in the walls or broken windows, or upended lamps on the floor. The place looked normal, basically. There was a pretty big crack in the glass of the coffee table, big enough that a chunk had broken off in the corner, but that's about it.

I don't know why, but this made me feel worse. It was like none of the usual things that blow up right before Mom is taken away had blown up. In which case, why hadn't we dealt with it ourselves? Why did the Christers have to be called this time? It's not like we don't know how to lock her in her room until she passes out. Something less obvious must have happened, some dark smoke must have risen up inside everybody and clouded their emotions with soot.

It was a mystery, and it would haunt me later, but right then, the important thing was that I go to Will and help him.

I crawled in behind him and wrapped my arms around him and rocked him gently back and forth. His muscles were so tense, like somebody had tied them into a thousand knots. Neither of us said anything for a long time. Eventually, his body softened and relaxed. He melted into me and let me hold him up. He was sobbing, long silent moans, and I just kept rocking him.

Whatever emotions I was feeling were manageable some-how, subdued. I was the one being strong this time, weirdly.

Eventually, his sobs leveled out into a wet, calm silence. He cleared his throat. "They're taking her to Hope Hill," he said. That's the rehab clinic up in the hills. She'd been there before. "She might be there for a couple months this time."

I absorbed this information without saying a word.

"Did you hear me?" he said.

I nodded into his shoulder. He was looking up at me now, and I noticed that he was cradling the trophy he'd won that day and that the golfer that was supposed to be standing on top of it had broken off somehow.

I felt bad for him. Worse even than I felt for me.

WILL

Ash was upset that they were taking Mom away again. I mean, I was too, but not in the same way. I was still sort of reeling from the fact that she'd attacked me. And even though I didn't trust the Christers—or Keith—to do much besides screw with her head, part of me thought, you know what? Maybe this is a good thing. Maybe once Mom realized how close she'd come to bludgeoning me, once she realized that she'd actually sliced me in the arm with my trophy—I thought this all might scare her straight or something.

But while she was gone, I understood, I'd have to take extra special care of Asheley. I'd be all she had. And she needed, you know, some sense of family, of normalcy in her life.

To be honest, I was pretty sure that she and I would be better in a whole lot of ways if it were just the two of us in the house.

So, that night while we sat on the floor of the living room decompressing and bolstering each other up, I tried to explain to her why sending Mom to Hope Hill might be a good idea.

I told her about the time Mom tried to run Dad over with the car once while he was putting up that old fence we used to have. He'd been standing in the middle of the driveway with the hose in his hand, like, spraying down the area where he'd been working. She'd gotten it into her head that he wasn't doing this to make the yard nicer like he'd claimed, but that, instead, he was doing this to trap her. Like turning the place into a prison or something so that she'd never be able to leave again. She reeled out of the house and into the station wagon and gunned it, headed straight at him. Dad hardly had time to realize what was happening. The hose went flying, whipping around like it had a bucking bronco trapped inside it, spraying water everywhere. Asheley and I came running out, not having any idea what was going on, but bawling our brains out anyway because we could tell, whatever it was, it was bad. And Dad's there straddling the front end of the car, his legs splayed out, his arms wrapped around the hood trying to get a firm grip, like he thinks he's Superman, able to bring her to a halt with pure force of will, skidding backward from the pressure of the car pushing into him, until he was almost right squashed up against the fence he'd just put up.

"She was so crazy angry at him that day," I told Asheley. "Just surging with anger, and when she tried to shift the car into overdrive, she put it into reverse instead. Then she gunned it again for the final deathblow, and she went slamming the other way into the garage door. I mean, it's just lucky he made it out of that situation alive."

And before you say it, I know. I know. I'm just like her. It's not like I got it from nowhere.

But, anyway. "Yeah," I said to Asheley, "good times. He pulled her out of the car and held her so tight that she couldn't move her arms, much less take a swing at him. And he just stood there with her like that until she exhausted herself and calmed down."

Talking about these sorts of things with Ash was tricky. She's got such an impossible idea of who Dad is. He was an action figure in Asheley's eyes. This big, strong shadowy presence that watched from a distance, waiting for the moment when she absolutely needed him. Then he'd swoop in and save her from all this.

I'm sure, even now, after everything that's happened, she still has these deluded ideas about him. When he used to come up, I always had to make sure that I didn't go crushing her fantasy of him. No matter how wrong it was. No matter how much I wanted to correct her and tell her exactly what kind of a total asshole he really was. I understood that she *needed* this fantasy. It gave her hope. And if I even tried to show her who he really was, she'd fly into a total panic. She'd yell at me, "Shut up! Shut up, shut up, shut up!" She just refused to hear it.

So while I was telling that story about Mom trying to run Dad over, I didn't mention that once he'd subdued her, he'd marched her up to their bedroom and locked her in, left her there for like a day and a half, even after she'd calmed down and no matter how much she begged and promised she'd get her anger under control. Yeah. He was quite a guy.

"I wish he was here now," she said. "He'd be way better than Keith at knowing what to do."

I almost lost it. Then I caught myself.

It's inevitable, I guess, that she'd idealize Dad. She never really knew the man. When he left, she was three years old. That's not a lot of time to get to know someone. And what you do know, you forget. I mean, I can't remember anything from when I was three, can you? Maybe a flash of sound, or the feeling of riding your Big Wheel down a hill, but that's about it. Nothing real. Nothing you can really get your head around.

Really, the only thing she remembers clearly is that he had a wiry brown beard that she liked to scratch her cheek against. Which is true. He did have a beard like that. Everything else, though? It's total bullshit.

Still, there's so little that's gone right in Asheley's life that I don't think I would have been able to live with myself if I'd stomped all over this fantasy of hers.

The truth is that I'm the one who's here to protect her. I'm the secret angel looking out for her. I always have been, I always will be.

She's okay, right?

Have you talked to her?

Tell me she's okay.

Or I can just stop talking.

Right. So, that night in the living room, after they took Mom away, things were bleak.

And the look on Asheley's face. Total fear of the future. And, see, here's a moment when I played the hero.

I cracked a smile. I winked at her. "Listen," I said, "I'll be right back." And I hopped up and ran up to my room to get the bottle of champagne I'd stashed away there last New Years, partly to keep it away from Mom, but also thinking that it would come in handy if I ever had anything to celebrate.

Holding the bottle high above my head, I took my time marching back down the stairs.

"Grab some glasses! We're gonna celebrate!" I said.

"Why?"

"First of all, I'm the best golfer in all of San Luis Obispo County. That counts for something. And second, you kicked ass today on the softball diamond. Right?"

"I guess so."

"So, you and I know how big that is. Why let Mom take our triumph away from us?"

"Ha." Asheley began to get into the spirit of things.

She set two wine glasses on the marble counter that separates the kitchen from the living room area and I positioned myself to pop the cork, aiming it toward the ceiling four floors above my head, toward the geometric, modernistic chandelier that Ash and I used to try to reach out and touch from the landing in front of our mother's room.

I twisted the metal wrapper off. I eased the cork up. And bang, like a gunshot, I sent it sailing. The second floor landing. Not bad for a first try.

Then I poured us each a glass, and holding mine up ready to toast, I said, "And, third, Mom's gone. She's gone! We're free! If that's not something to celebrate, I don't know what is!"

"You think so?"

"Absolutely! Hell, if we can survive life with her in the house, we can definitely survive life without her!

This got a timid grin out of her.

We chinked glasses and drank.

"Wonder Twins, unite!" I said, and we touched our fists together.

God that was satisfying. Just saying it aloud, *Mom, I don't need you.* It was like suddenly I really was free, like I wasn't just pretending for Asheley's sake.

And with my emotions running high like they were, I drank fast. We both did. We finished the bottle off in maybe an hour, tops. We put some music on and cranked it up loud—not Mom's crusty old Guns N' Roses, but good music. Our music. And we danced around, spazzing out. It was fantastic. In some weird way, we were purging ourselves of Mom. The longer we danced, the lighter the room got, like her mean spirit was going up in smoke.

Finally, exhausted, we collapsed to the floor and laid there on the rug, watching the room spin around us.

"Hey, remember that game we used to play?" I said. "Out by the cliffs? When we'd sit at the edge and let our feet dangle off the side?"

"End of the World!"

"Yes! End of the World! And we'd imagine what was lurking down there, all that stuff we couldn't see because the fog was so thick. You always said popsicles."

"Well, yeah, of course, because at the edge of the world there's another one, and in that one everything *is* made of popsicles. Don't you know anything, Will?"

"Everything? Popsicles? Don't you think the roads would be made of ice cream sandwiches, at least?"

"Nope. . . . I guess maybe there's some creamsicles, but they're sort of the odd ducks. They don't get along with all the popsicle everything else." Then she kicked me with her heel. "You know what else I remember?" she said. "You got mad one day and threw my Barbie off the cliff."

"Yeah, but that was to prove a point! You didn't believe things could survive the leap from this world to the next and I had to show you they could. I climbed down immediately, through the fog and everything, and I'm telling you, it was treacherous, I couldn't see a thing, and I got that Barbie back for you."

"You got her back, but her face was smashed in!"

"Well, she survived, though."

"Barely."

"Enough to torture Ken for another five years."

"Ha!" she said.

We laid there, sort of floating, almost content, filled with hope.

"Ash?" I said. I'd been thinking about the way she fantasized about Dad, thinking I should let her know, somehow, that I was the one she should really rely on.

"Ash, we don't need anyone else. Really. Ever. I swear, I promise, I'll protect you. For the rest of your life. No matter what happens."

ASHELEY

I'm at the mercy of my moods. If I'm in a dark place, like I was then, it takes an immense amount of effort for me to force myself out of it. What I mean is, I missed Craig. Even after what had happened. I wanted to see him, to talk to him. He had his own problems with family, and I just knew talking to him would make me feel better. But I didn't want to seem desperate about it.

Among the many things I had let slide since that night when everything went down with Mom was that I hadn't spoken to him. He'd sent me a couple texts, one on Sunday saying, *What's up?* then another a day later saying, *You still pissed?* but I sort of didn't have the nerve to text him back.

Like I said, I was having serious trouble dealing.

So, when Naomi called me on Wednesday morning to see if I was still going to Becca's party, I said "Absolutely! I've been looking forward to it all week," not 'cause I wanted to go, exactly, but 'cause I didn't want to not go. It seemed like an important thing to do. To prove to myself I was still capable of being a human being, somehow.

WILL

Becca's party?

Yeah, that was a kind of early tip off.

I told Ash not to go.

I said, "The only reason you're going is to show them you can. To prove to them that you're not afraid of them. But you don't like those people. They're all a bunch of Joiners. You don't need those people. What do you care if they think you're afraid or not? Stay here and watch old episodes of *Lost* on Hulu with me. That's what you really want to do."

But did she listen to me?

Of course not.

ASHELEY

So, the party:

Naomi gave me a ride, and the first thing, she was disappointed that Will wasn't coming. I had to make up a lie. "Oh, he's sick," I said. "Food poisoning. He ate some bad chicken."

She arched an eyebrow. "He's not just avoiding me?"

"No, of course not. He wanted to come. He just . . . he's been vomiting for the past four hours."

"Ugh," she said. "Well, he's not off the hook. That boy needs to be socialized!"

Right, I know, you want to hear about Craig. I'll get to what happened with him. There's a few steps in between I have to explain, though.

We got to Becca's house and the place was so jam-packed that we had to park like a block and a half away and walk up the hill. Then when we got inside, it took almost half an hour to push through the crowd crammed around the drinks table.

By the time I got out of the thick of the mob, Naomi had disappeared.

I wandered into the backyard to check things out. It was just like I'd heard. This massive landscaped place with lots of separate areas to it—the hot tub area, the pool area, the orchard area, the grotto area—each held up on a different level by a wall of blond rocks. It was like something out of Epcot Center or something, uber-rich America land.

I toured through each area, sort of keeping to myself, exploring. Craig didn't seem to be there, and that was a huge disappointment. Finally I found a quiet spot on the back porch where I could sort of be alone. I figured, if I could hang out here for a while and get used to being in this big social space, I'd be able to catch the spirit of the fun and eventually relax enough to join in.

A few of the softball girls found me eventually—Crystal, Ruth—and we chatted for a while and then Ruth said, "Hey, did you and Craig break up or something? What's up with him?"

A shot of panic went rumbling through me.

"What do you mean? Is he here? Where?" I said.

"Of course he's here," she said. "It's not a party if Craig hasn't shown up." Then she gave me a crooked look. "Sort of defensive, aren't we, Asheley?"

"Yeah, it's just—"

"Trouble in paradise?"

"No, no, it's just . . . I didn't know he'd gotten here yet. Where is he?"

She pointed across the yard, and there he was with Pauly, sitting high up on one of the stone walls. They'd brought bright red-and-yellow pump action water guns with them and were shooting people in the back of the head.

Seeing him, I totally lost my nerve. I circled around to a spot near the trees where, hopefully, I could see him but he couldn't see me.

He and Pauly were targeting girls. Aiming for their butts. And then when the girl would spin and look for who shot her, they'd wiggle their fingers at her in a way that was goofy and threatening all at the same time. Lewd in some hard to explain way.

I couldn't help wondering if he knew I was there. He always seemed to be situated in just such a way as to almost, but not quite, be looking at me.

Yeah, it rattled me. It made me a little paranoid. He seemed fine without me. Oblivious. Not missing me at all. And the better off he seemed, the more I wondered what was wrong with me.

And then, almost like I'd willed her into being, Claudia Jackson came dancing up to me! Claudia Jackson! Completely drunk—like bombed off her ass, which I guess is no surprise. She's got that rep. She's the girl people invite out to parties just to see what kind of fool she'll turn into this time. She was wearing a horrible lime-green bikini underneath a button-down shirt that she'd tied to show off her boobs. This was supposed to be a seductive look, I think, but the effect was it highlighted her belly rolls.

"Hey, Asheley," she said, "I'd start protecting my assets, if I were you. Craig's totally flirting with every girl here."

Of course it made me angry! But that doesn't . . . It made

me sad, too. Mostly sad. What I did was flee. I followed the cobblestone path up the hill and perched myself against a broken Grecian column in the ruins area way up in the highest plane. From there, I could see basically everything, and in order to distract myself from Craig, I tried to find other things to pay attention to. People were jumping in and out of the pool, lounging around in the hot tub, smoking up in the shadows where they thought they couldn't be seen. Becca and her brothers were wandering around with cookie sheets filled with Dixie Cups of Day-Glo blue and yellow Jell-O shots. Groups of girls were falling all over each other in the folding chairs Becca had set up everywhere, posing in groups for photo after photo to post to their Facebook pages, as though getting drunk was some huge accomplishment. Guys were standing in packs along the edges of the action, checking out the girls, tilting their whole bodies to comment to each other, then laughing in huffy self-satisfied ways.

A shot of water hit me in the gut, and turning to see where it had come from, I saw Craig far below me, bobbing in the pool, waving his gun in the air like an action hero.

And who was there with him? Claudia, the skank. She had her legs wrapped around his waist, one arm thrown over his shoulder, half floating in the water, half grinding up against him.

He grinned at me. "Sucka!" he shouted, a gaping, drooling drunken grin taking over his entire face.

They kissed. Well, she kissed him and he let her do it. And the only thing I could think to do was call Will and ask him to come rescue me.

WILL

If you only knew what kind of a rage I was in. I leapt out of the car almost before I'd turned it off, before I even knew what he'd done to her, and I raced off to find him. I swear, I could have killed him right there. That's all I kept thinking. That no way was I going to let him hurt Asheley like this.

But, and this is important, you have to understand, even after all this, Ash wanted to protect him. She grabbed me by the edge of my shirt and yanked me back. Actually tore the shirt. She begged me to leave him alone. That's when the tears came. They were like a tidal wave. She kept mumbling, "Let's just go. Take me home. Right now. Take me home. Please. Right now. Right now. Right now."

So, okay, fine. I took her home.

She wouldn't say one word about what had happened. It's

not like I couldn't figure it out. I said to her, "I could give two shits if he was drunk. So what? That doesn't excuse him." I was speeding. Flooring it. "Did he touch you?" I said. "He must have touched you. Is that it, Ash? Did he try to hurt you? Like, physically? Try to rip off your skirt?"

So, yeah, I was completely out of control. But wouldn't you be? I mean . . .

We must have been going close to eighty by then. Yanking a left turn, I spun us around so quick that the Explorer went up on two wheels, almost toppled over. We went up on the median, then bounced back down. I looked up and next thing I knew, we were barreling right toward the light post. I slammed on the brakes and we screeched to a halt, I swear, not even an inch from hitting the damn thing.

We sat there for a second.

"It's not like he raped me," Asheley said quietly. "It's stupid. He was kissing some skanky girl. I shouldn't even care."

"But you still do care."

"Well, wouldn't you?"

"I don't know. Yeah, I guess, maybe. But"—I took her hand—"you shouldn't. You're way too good for him," I said.

"You think so?" she said.

"Definitely."

A whisper of a smile invaded her face, like she wasn't sure if it was okay to feel a little better about herself.

Holding my fist up for her to tap, I said, "Wonder Twin powers!"

"Unite!" she said.

We bumped fists.

The light had gone from green to red to green again.

"So, home?" she said.

"Yeah, I'm waiting for the light." As it turned yellow, I began a countdown. "Five, four, three, two, one." It went red, and I gunned it and we raced across the intersection.

That made her laugh.

The rest of the way home, I felt so at peace, such a sense of accomplishment. I'd never experienced a peace like that before. Like I could handle anything. Me and Ash. It was . . . I can't even explain it.

ASHELEY

After that, things were pretty okay for a while. I mean, I was still sad about how things had ended up with Craig, but I was able to contain it. I didn't do anything stupid or dramatic. I didn't call him or text him or anything. I just sort of let it ride and kept to myself.

I was living my life. Going to Milky Moo's, the ice cream shop on our one main shopping street where I'd gotten a summer job. Coming home. Watching TV with Will, or sometimes just watching him play *Halo*. On days when I wasn't working, I'd set myself up on a beach chair in the backyard and sunbathe all day, listening to my iPod and reading.

It was nice. Simple. I'd make small talk with Mrs. Stein, who owned the store, when she stopped by to make sure everything was okay. I'd smile and pretend to be content, happy, whenever someone from school popped in for a cone. I'd walk back and forth from home—we weren't that far really, maybe a mile or so—and try to convince myself I didn't need more than this.

And then, this one evening—it must have been about a week after Becca's party—I was closing out Milky Moo's, shutting down the soft-serve machines and counting the money in the register and soaking the scoopers and everything, and it all sort of hit me at once, so forcefully that I got dizzy and had to sit down for a minute. How normal things were. Even though Mom was locked up in Hope Hill and Keith was out there with her, staying at a Motel 8 down the road so he could check in on her every day, things were normal.

Will and I were cooking dinner every night—easy stuff like pasta from the jar and Hot Pockets and such, but still—trying not to spend more than the budget Keith and Mom had provided us with. We'd even been doing chores, cleaning the house, mowing the lawn, all that sort of thing.

Like I said, normal. And the thing that confused me, the thing that got me so discombobulated that I had to sit down to stop myself from fainting, was that it seemed like I hadn't known what normal was until then. Normal was the thing that was weird to me, if that makes sense. And I distinctly remember thinking, "So this is what life would have been like if Mom hadn't driven Dad away like she did."

That was the day we decided to have our party.

When I got home from work, Will was in the kitchen, hunkered over the counter, already making dinner.

"Hi, honey," I called out to him. "I'm home." We'd started having fun like that. It was like playing house.

"Masheley potatoes!" he said with a grin. He hadn't called me that in years.

"Whatcha cooking?" I asked, heading into the kitchen area. "Smells spicy."

He'd covered every inch of counter space with piles of ingredients. Sour cream, grated cheese, tortillas, salsa. He'd opened a can of beans and chopped up some lettuce and tomatoes. He was even cooking up some ground beef to throw in there.

"Tacos?" I said. "Burritos?"

"Mexican surprise," he said, picking a dish towel off the counter and flicking it at me. "Don't you worry about it." Then he pulled a blender full of lime slush out of the freezer. "Here. Have a margarita and stop distracting the chef."

He poured a drink for me, and placing a hand on each of my shoulders, marched me into the living room and plopped me onto the couch.

"Your job is to sit here and watch TV. Drink your margarita. Do nothing for a while. You've been working all day. I've been hanging out playing *Halo*. I'll set up a TV tray and serve you when it's ready."

"Well, okay. If you're demanding it."

While I watched Colbert on the DVR, I rotated my arm trying to keep it loose. That ice cream in the freezer box is hard as a rock and eight hours of sculpting it into balls tears you up. My shoulder was killing me, which was weird because I would have thought playing softball would build up those muscles. I guess not. Different muscles.

It was nice, having a drink and letting Will wait on me. I was thinking I could get used to this.

Will put the plate in front of me—which was great, by the way: a gargantuan, overstuffed burrito, with sour cream and guacamole on top and everything.

Oh, and Keith showed up too, that night. Will and I shot each other a look.

He walked right in, left the front door open and everything and headed straight for the fridge, almost like it was his house, which it isn't. He might hang around all the time when Mom's here, but he actually lives in a beat-up old houseboat down at the docks.

"Keith, come on in. Make yourself at home," Will said. I don't think Keith got the sarcasm because he just stroked his braid and gazed at Will through his giant glasses. Sort of lurking.

"Your mom sent me to get some CDs for her," he said, eventually. "And her cowboy boots, she wants those too." But he didn't make a move, just kept standing there. I think maybe he was stoned. That was the trade off. He didn't drink anymore, but he still let himself smoke pot because, he said, pot was "healthful."

"You guys doing okay?" he said, finally.

"Yeah, uh-huh, fine," I said. Enough nodding and smiling and you could usually get him to wander off after a while. Really, Keith was kind of like a dimwitted old dog sometimes. He'd sniff at you, get confused, and go on his way.

"You're cooking," he said. "Partaking of the bounty of the earth."

"Something like that, yeah," said Will. He was getting

annoyed. I could tell. His leg was bouncing like it does when he gets anxious.

Keith nosed around the kitchen, poking and sniffing at the things Will had left out. "A lot of cans," he said. "Maybe you're not so much partaking of the bounty of the earth. Looks more like the bounty of the corporation."

"It's food," Will said. "Food is food."

"But all food's not created equal. You're cooking though, that's step one. You're breaking the frozen food, TV dinner cycle. But you've got that whole garden I planted out back there. Fresh basil and cilantro and heirloom tomatoes. Next time I pop by I'll give you some tips."

Will, over-sensitive as always, was stung by this. He started pounding out a rhythm on his knee. His focus turned inward. He'd spent hours making this special meal for me, and even if it was just Keith making fun of it, the criticism was enough to flick a speck of self-doubt into his feeling of accomplishment.

I took a huge bite and smacked my lips and said, "I don't care if it's not organic from our personal garden. It's still really good. What matters is the love you put into it."

I stuck my tongue out at Will and he cracked a smile.

"Well, then I better try it," said Keith. He started opening cabinets in search of a plate.

"No way, man. No fucking way." Will leapt up and raced to the kitchen to protect his creation. "You're going to have to go get takeout from the macrobiotic shop downtown."

"Yeah," I called, through a mouthful of burrito. "Go get some tofu. This processed crap will kill you."

"What are you doing here anyway, Keith? You're obviously not here to get Mom's cowboy boots. I visited her last time she was in Hope Hill. They don't allow shoes there. They make you walk around barefoot. Shouldn't you be reading girlie mags on your houseboat or something?"

This got a smirk out of Keith. "I figured you might need a responsible adult to stop by every once in a while, make sure you're still breathing and all that," he said.

"A responsible adult? Let me know if you find one of them. I'd like to meet him."

I couldn't help it: I cracked up when Will said this.

Keith raised his hands above his head like we'd caught him stealing and started backing up toward the door. "No worries, dudes," he said. "I'm around if you need me, cool?"

"Yeah, Keith. Cool," Will said.

"Till then, I'll catch you on the flip side."

A loose-limbed wave, and he was off.

Will flopped down on the couch next to me. "Jesus!" he said.

"Yeah, but you were amazing." I hit him playfully in the arm. "My protector."

I think this made him blush. Anyway, he wouldn't let me see his face; he sort of held it up and away from me for a while.

So, then we finished dinner and zapped on the tube and gorged ourselves on three, was it? Four? Maybe five hours of *Criminal Minds*. I curled up on the couch and put my head in his lap. Sometimes one of us would say something and we'd talk for a second then fade back into the show. It was an odd experience. Just sort of being, in that totally normal way that wasn't actually normal at all.

"I feel like a person, in this weird way," I said to him after it got late and it seemed like we'd be shuffling off to bed soon.

"Yeah?"

"Yeah. Like a grown-up or something. Like a person with a life."

Which is when it occurred to me: let's have a dinner party. Isn't that the sort of thing grown-ups do?

The idea made Will nervous. I could feel his muscles tensing up. But he wasn't saying no.

"Really?" he said. "Didn't you get enough of the Joiners last week?"

"I'm not talking about a rager. Just a dinner party. And you could cook and we could drink red wine and talk about fine art and current events," I said.

"Who would we invite?"

"I don't know. Definitely not Craig. We'd only invite people who deserve to come. Maybe four or five people? We'll think about it and make a list. Naomi. That's one."

"Naomi? Really?"

"What's wrong with Naomi?"

"She's so proud of herself all the time."

"She's cooler than you think. Also"—I wasn't sure if I should mention this, but I figured why not, it might get him a little more jazzed about the idea—"I'm pretty sure she's got a crush on you. She definitely wants to hook up with you."

"I don't know," he said. "I guess we could try it."

"And Naomi?" I said.

He cracked a half-smirk. "Do *you* think I should like Naomi?"

"Absolutely," I said.

I don't know what else I can tell you. It seemed like a good idea at the time.

WILL

No, I didn't invite anybody. Who would I have asked? The golf team? They're a bunch of douche bags. And who else was there? Other kids from school? I hated those people. They might have forgotten all the times they'd smashed my head into my locker and thrown the dodge ball at my nuts during gym class and all that crap they used to do to me, but I hadn't.

You know, one time, I was in chemistry class. This was, like, sophomore year, and we were making some sort of dangerous concoction. You mixed the chemicals and they went from green to purple and then the beaker filled up with smoke. The kind of thing that you had to wear your goggles and rubber gloves to do because if it spilled on you, it might burn through your hands. And this prick, Andy Berman—a real straitlaced kid, like, all As and cardigans and hair that looked like it had been parted with a shovel—Andy Berman, and his lab partner Jen Letts—who got teased herself all the time because people thought her last name made her a whore somehow—the two of them started whispering and snickering to each other and Andy says loud enough for the whole class to hear, "Hey, I bet this stuff is strong enough to clear up Baird's zits!" Har, har. Everybody gets a big kick out of that one. So, fine, I'd been hearing crap like that forever. Who cares. Not me. I did care, though, when Mr. Lewison stepped out of the room and they all started chasing me around with it, like, pinning me down and holding their beakers over my face so that the only thing stopping it from burning my skin off was the rubber stopper. Fuck yeah, I minded that.

So, no. I had no interest in inviting anybody. Thanks, no. I don't think so.

But Asheley wanted to have some people over, so I said, "Okay. If it makes you happy, we'll have some people over."

She had said there'd be five of them. Girls from the softball team. I can't remember who. Naomi and a few of the others. They were friends of Asheley's, that's all that mattered.

I tried, though, that night. I really did. I made lasagna, a salad from Keith's garden. We broke out some frozen jalapeño poppers and mini egg rolls for appetizers. Ash got us ice cream from Milky Moo's. Fine. I was all down for playing the good host and smiling and pretending this was fun for me.

Ha. Some dinner party. Exactly what I didn't want to happen happened.

Eight o'clock, eight thirty came and we started getting all kinds of knocks on the door. The girls from the softball team.

Then, the baseball team. And the track team. Hell, even the chess team showed up. Guess someone didn't get the memo.

They took over the stereo. There was pounding music and a massive grayish noise bouncing around the room from everybody shouting. There were people spilling their beer all over the hardwood floors.

Just . . . not a dinner party. More like a *let's all get shit-faced* Joiner party.

And I couldn't find Asheley.

And I kept getting caught up by Naomi. She'd grin at me and say things like, "Hey, let's do some shots! I know how to make this great thing called a Swedish Fish," or "This house is crazy weird. It's like an aquarium. Where are all the other rooms? Can I get a tour?" or "When's your next tournament? You're going to State, now, right?" Just grinning and grinning. I'd mumble something to her and she'd nod and grin some more. Why? Because she liked me? She didn't like me! She didn't even know me. She hadn't known me since we were in fifth grade, when we'd sat next to each other in Mrs. Kelly's class and she would pass me all these stupid notes all the time, like, what's your favorite color, and do you like music, and if you were an animal, which animal would you be? That's the last time we'd ever had a real conversation. So, it was annoying and sort of horrifying to have her acting all buddy-buddy with me now.

And meanwhile, more and more people are streaming in. The golf team, now. Lewis and Ricardo. It was like somebody had posted a Facebook event: Come ruin Will's night—Saturday—his house!

I finally said to Naomi, "Look, can you lay off, just for a minute? I've got to find my sister. I need to ask her something." I tried to be as nice as I could about it. It's just, I had to find out if this was just a spontaneous event, people passing the word around until critical mass, or if I should be angry specifically at Ash.

Turns out she was in the kitchen, jamming frozen pizzas into the oven. She was surrounded by a whole mess of girls from her team, and I could tell from the way she was spazzing around that she was anxious about making sure she appreciated them.

She flashed me a smile. "Hey bro," she said.

"Hey bro, yourself," I hissed. Then I leaned in to whisper so I wouldn't embarrass her. "Who are all these people?" I said.

Her answer came loud. "They're party people, Will! It's a par-tay!" She'd had a few drinks, clearly.

I kept my composure and whispered, "Tell me you didn't invite every Joiner in school."

"Of course not. It just happened. But . . . are you angry?" The thought alarmed her, but at least she got the hint that I was serious. Whispering herself, now, she said, "The only people I invited were the ones on our list. I don't know where all the rest of these people came from."

"Well, Lewis and Ricardo just walked in. We don't have enough lasagna for all these people."

"Dude," she said, playing to the crowd again. "The lasagna ran out like an hour ago. People loved it." She hip-checked me and winked. "Relax, Will. It's a party. Our party. You and me. These are our friends. Work with me, you know?"

So, what was I supposed to do with that? I guess she wanted to have a blowout after all.

"Go with it," I said back to her. "Yeah."

You're right. I was sort of pissed. And sort of panicky. But Asheley seemed happy so . . . I mean, I was trying to deal, you know? To just get through it.

I did what I always do in situations like this when I'm uncomfortable and under assault. I withdrew. I slipped out of the house. I got my driver and a basket of balls from the shed out back and walked into the darkness, took the path through the forest to my place on the rocks, and I stood out there hitting balls off the edge of the cliff, watching them sail out over the bay and then drop, watching the water swallow them up, trying to calm myself down, and thinking how great it would be to dive in, to just dive in and be done with everything.

ASHELEY

It must have been about eleven when Craig called. Eleven thirty, maybe.

And I picked up. Why? I was a little buzzed. Not drunk, not sloppy or anything, but riding a wave of good feeling, dancing barefoot in my own living room, surrounded by all the coolest kids in school. All these people who, it turned out, liked me a whole lot more than I'd ever imagined. It was like the world was tilting toward a happier place. And I saw Craig's name come up on my screen and I didn't even think about my anger toward him, I just thought, hey, Craig's calling, let's see what he wants.

It wasn't until I actually heard his voice that I realized, oh, it's Craig. The last person on earth I want to deal with.

"Can we talk?" he said.

I sobered up just like that. I ducked out of the cluster of people I'd been dancing with and slipped out the sliding door onto the back porch. It was quieter there. The party was all taking place inside the house. "We're talking now. I answered, didn't I?"

"But can we talk for real?" he said. "Or are you going to hate me no matter what I say?"

"That depends on what you say, doesn't it?"

"I feel like total shit."

"Well, you should."

"I know."

"Oh, do you?"

"Yeah. I'm an asshole. I know it. You have no idea how completely I know it."

"I think I do, actually."

"All I've done, for like a week now, the single thing I've been able to do is wake and bake and sit there and . . ." He sounded like he was about to cry. The last thing I needed, right about then. "Just sit there. You know? Thinking about what a dick I am and how I totally messed up the one thing I've ever wanted to do right."

Wow. I could feel myself getting sucked into the mud. I got hot flashes of details of all the good and bad times I'd had with him—our first kiss, out behind the bluff at the edge of the bay where I'd been watching him surf that morning, the tingling anticipation that came after, all that not knowing and hoping he really liked me, then the conversations we'd had, these deep, deep conversations, all my secrets and all my insecurities and all my sadnesses dished out for him to stomp on if he wanted.

Inside, the dancing continued. The muffled bass line of a

hip-hop song was pulsing through the door. Will was wedged into the nook under the stairs, propped on a stepladder, watching everybody bop around. He had a kind of terrified expression on his face, like, shell-shocked, like he wished he could melt into the wall, get as far away from these people as possible. I wondered, briefly, if maybe this party wasn't such a good idea. Naomi was bouncing around on the other side of the glass and she caught my eye and threw me a quizzical look. I shook her off. This stuff with Craig was private. I'd kept it that way so far and no way was I going to change that now.

"Craig, you know I'm having a party, right? You must know. The whole school knows. The eighth graders at RFK probably know. You really want to do this now? I should be in there hosting. Or is that the point?"

"That's not the point, Ash. I'm not trying to ruin your good vibe. Give me at least a little credit, huh?"

"Then, what? Isn't there a better time to do this?"

"Can I just see you? For five minutes? That's all. Then I'll leave."

"Wait, what? Leave?" It was like my stomach had just dropped out of my body. "Are you here? Are you totally insane, Craig?"

"Yeah. I mean, sort of. Not exactly. I just, I couldn't take it anymore. I biked over. I had to get out of the house. I had to try to see you."

"You're here? At my party? Right now? After all the ways you've—"

"Asheley, wait! Wait! That's not what I mean. I'm not that stupid."

"Then—"

"I'm out on the curb. Like around the corner near the woods. That's partly why I'm calling. To ask your permission to let me in?"

From my spot on the back porch, I could see the woods and I knew just where he would have been balanced on his bike—at the place where the road curved in toward the cliffs—but it was too dark. The pines were too thick to see anything that might be going on out there.

"What happens if I say no?" I said.

"I don't know. I'll go home, I guess. And sit there. And think about all the ways I've fucked everything up. I'll tell you what I won't do. I won't bother you ever again."

And what did I do? I said. "Fine, five minutes. Not one more."

I remember wondering at the time why I was doing this. I've thought about it a lot since then, too, maybe even every day, and I still don't know. Maybe I didn't trust that he was telling the truth and I wanted to head him off before he burst into the house and made a scene in front of everybody. The thought crossed my mind. But I don't know, maybe it was something else—the threat of him never speaking to me again. Maybe no matter how over him I wanted to be, I still loved him. Maybe I wanted to forgive him.

Saying a secret goodbye to my party, I sort of hopped into the woods and took the shortcut out toward the road. Remember, I'd been dancing. I was barefoot. I kept stepping on pebbles and pine cones and twigs.

When I came out of the trail, I was maybe fifteen, twenty feet behind him. I have to admit, he was sort of adorable, hunched over his BMX, his hair standing up every which way, like he just couldn't get it to go right by himself. He was staring up the road toward the globes at the end of my driveway, waiting for me to appear in the light. He'd actually put on a shirt for the occasion, a short-sleeved, baby-blue-and-gray pattern button-down with a Chinese dragon curling around the waist.

"Hey," I said, padding toward him.

He startled. "Oh, hey. I thought—" His arms twisting and darting around each other, he pointed toward the light.

"I know. I took the shortcut."

To get away from the gravel along the side of the road, I stood on the pavement and made sure to keep three or four feet distance between us. Neither of us knew what to say. He kept trying on different versions of his smile to see which one would get a positive reaction, but no matter how much I wanted to, I wasn't budging.

"Thanks for coming out," he said, finally.

"Yeah, well. Like I said, five minutes." I pointed at the place where my watch would be if I wore one. "More like four and a half now."

"I missed you."

"I find that hard to believe."

"Don't be like that." He reached for my waist and tried to coax me toward him but I pushed his hand away.

"Why shouldn't I be like that? It seems to me you've been a little busy to miss me."

"What? No!" He reached for my waist again.

"With Claudia? At Becca's party?"

"Are you kidding? Ash . . . no, Ash—"

"Don't give me that, Craig. You know I saw you. You sprayed me with your squirt gun to make sure of it."

"I didn't do anything with Claudia Jackson! Asheley, come on! She's Claudia Jackson! She was just convenient! She was just there! And I saw you and you were doing everything you could to stay aloof and I sort of went crazy, Ash, really. Why do you think I squirted you? You think I'd work that hard to get your attention if I was really hooking up with Claudia Jackson?"

"Looked like it to me."

"You were supposed to get jealous. That's all that was going on. I thought if you got jealous you might at least tell me off, and that would mean, at least, that you still cared about me a little. But then, no, you ran off. I spent the rest of the party trying to find you. Really. Claudia disgusts me. I got away from her as fast as I could."

With that sad look tugging at his face, how could I not believe him? The things he was saying made too much sense, they clicked too well with everything I knew about him to be lies. He was macho and insecure and even when he wasn't trying to get to me, ninety percent of what he did in public was just showing off, just performing for the crowd. Which doesn't mean I liked it.

"Do you think that was respectful?" I asked him.

"No." He was glum. Contrite. He looked like a little boy, like he was eight years old again, waiting urgently for his mom to reprimand him.

"I mean, Craig, don't you think the better thing to do would have been to come up and talk to me?"

His body spasmed with emotion. "I'm doing that now!"

"Yeah, now after torturing me for two weeks."

"I'm sorry!" he said, pleading, holding his hands out to me palm up like I was a goddess and he was begging me for my blessing.

I softened. I couldn't help it. All that power in my hands made me uncomfortable. I like peace. I want everyone to feel . . . safe. And I don't trust myself to be as kind as I should. The thought . . . the thought that I might hurt someone I cared about . . . no matter how deeply they've hurt me . . .

I'm sorry. I shouldn't be crying. I don't know why I'm crying. Can't we just skip this part? It . . .

I can try, but . . .

I said to Craig, very quietly, "I know. I know you're sorry, really, I do. But—" This was hard for me. Asserting myself. He had to understand though. "You can't do that, what you did at Shakey's, I mean. You know? It's not fair. I'm a person, not a sex doll. And that was such an important day for me. I'd accomplished something. All those girls, they'd accepted me. I needed to *have* that."

This time when he reached for me, I let him take my hands. We were looking straight into each other's eyes. I could feel him taking in the things I was saying. Completely. His macho and pride were totally gone. He was filling himself up with me. With my needs.

"Just because you want to hook up doesn't mean I do too all the time. And just because I say no, not right now, doesn't mean I don't like you anymore. You've got to—sometimes I just need some space, you know? I—"

Squeezing my fingers, he cut me off. "I get it Ash. I get it, okay? I'm a dick. It's all I've been able to think about. I'm a total asshole. You're right. I'm wrong. I know that. You know? I'm a lug head. It's just . . . you're so fucking sexy! I don't know what happens to me. I see you and I just can't stop myself. I want to start humping your leg or something. Even if I know how wrong it is. I can't help it. Everything else drops out of my mind and it's just, *Asheley, Asheley, Asheley*, and your skin and your curves—and you're right, I should learn to control myself. Kick me a few times. Don't put up with it. I'll get the hint eventually. But . . ."

He let go of my hands and dropped his head. He took a deep breath that caught in his throat like a hiccup. Was he crying? It seemed like he was crying. Or about to cry. He was trembling. Doing everything he possibly could to stop the tears from rolling down his face.

He mumbled, "I love you, Asheley." I could barely hear the words they were so soft.

And I wanted so badly to believe him. Even though I wasn't sure if I still loved him, or if I loved him enough, or if he was good for me in any way, even though I knew nothing would really change, he'd still run around like a loon, goofing on everything, creating chaos like a kid playing in the mud, even though it was abundantly clear to me that I couldn't count on him no matter how much I wished I could, even though I knew it was the last thing I should be doing at the moment, I leaned in and kissed him, a soft peck on the lips.

"I think I love you too," I said.

"You're not sure?"

"No," I said.

Then he kissed me again, a little longer this time.

And again. The tips of our tongues touched.

And again.

He had his arms around my waist, pulling me into him, his hands sliding everywhere.

I don't know if I wanted that. I don't know. Maybe I wanted it. It freaked me out, I think.

I wanted to kiss him, yeah, but . . .

We toppled off his bike and rolled into the grassy ditch along the side of the road.

His hands slid up under my shirt and played across my stomach, and he pushed me back and rolled on top of me. He caught me in the ribs with his elbow and I let out a yelp of pain. I was struggling, I think. It was hard to breathe under him.

Look, can we stop this? I don't . . . I, really, I can't do this.

Fine, okay. At some point, I screamed. There was something rustling in the woods, too. Maybe I was freaked out because Craig was hurting me, or maybe it was the sound. I don't know. This all happened so fast. It's all mashed up together.

I pushed at Craig's chest, tried to push him off me. He was heavy—and strong—and I couldn't get out from under him.

And then this shadow shot out of the trees and it was Will, and he was shouting, "Get off her, you fuck, get the fuck off her," and Craig started pulling and yanking at me. To protect me? To stop me from getting away? I don't know. He was shouting now too, they were both shouting, everyone was shouting, and the more I flailed, the more tightly Craig held me. I pushed and I punched and I clawed at Craig's face and my finger got twisted in the leather strap that he wore around his neck, the one that held the green-and-black ceramic bead he liked, the one I bought for him—it had a hand-painted infinity sign on it—and as I flailed, the strap snapped and got tangled in my hand and . . . and I was free somehow.

And I ran.

And that's it. That's all I remember. Okay? I ran back to the party.

Can you, please, can you stop pushing me on this? It's horrible enough without you pushing me.

Or, I can just stop talking altogether. We can do that, too.

Okay, thank you.

WILL

The sound. That's what I remember most. The sound of the driver coming down on his head. Like the popping of a nutshell, but wetter. When I heard that sound, I realized, suddenly, what I'd done. The whole world stopped for a second and a spike of horror plummeted through me. I think I was in shock.

Please. You don't have to show me the photo again. I already told you I did it. But you have to understand, he was trying to rape her!

I knew he was dead. No way he couldn't be. It was ugly. Him lying down, now, his legs twisted under him, his neck thrown back like he was about to scream. But he wasn't screaming. He wasn't making a sound. Blood seeping into the thick bed of pine needles underneath his skull. Me, standing over him, the driver limp in my hand, its head sticky with blood, twitching with every slight movement of my hand.

I started walking, still in a daze, not sure where I was going. Slowly. Meandering. Like I was drunk. I reached up to swat a mosquito on my forehead and when I looked at my hand, I saw it was smeared with blood. I don't think I really understood it, that I was capable of this, that it had actually happened, until I saw the blood smeared across my hand like that.

Then things started moving again, real fast. The rage revved up inside my chest again, and I felt justified, righteous, glad that I'd done it. I hadn't had a choice. He'd been attacking Asheley— mauling her—taking advantage of her weakness and her good heart, her heart that forgives and forgives and accepts the blame no matter who's wrong. She couldn't defend herself. No way. Not if she'd wanted to. I saw that. She'd been screaming, pushing to get away, and he'd just kept grunting and forcing himself on her. I had to protect her. I was the only one who'd ever been able to protect her. And if I didn't do so now. . . . Like I said, I had absolutely no choice. I couldn't just stand there and watch her get raped. What did she know about sex and love? Nothing. She was still filled with fantasies about princesses and rainbows. A good girl. That's what she was. Innocent and fragile and beautiful—but naive, trusting, even when she shouldn't be. And no way could I let Craig take advantage of this. No way. No way could I let him stomp over her body, take it to wear as a pelt on his sword. That kid. He had a rep. He'd done it before. Chelsea Sullivan. Theresa Gomez. He was a virgin slayer. He broke them and left them like roadkill for the coyotes to gnaw on. I couldn't let that happen. Not to Asheley I couldn't. I couldn't let him turn her into our mother.

It was self-defense. That's how I figured it. What else could it be? Asheley's my sister, an extension of myself, and he was attacking her. Self-defense.

I shot her a text: *Where are u?! Need to talk! Desperately!*

But I got no reply.

In my wandering, I'd ended up landing at the edge of the backyard, at the mouth of the trail, kneeling at the cusp of the light from the house, watching all those fools tromping around the house. The Joiners. They were dancing. Bopping up and down, flailing their arms. Oblivious as ever.

I returned to the road to get Craig's bike and then snuck it the long way around the house and hid it in the shed—it was dark enough back there for me to do that.

And then I sat there in the shadows for what seemed like forever, watching, waiting for everyone to leave. Once in a while, I saw Asheley flit by, and my heart would jump and I'd pray all over again that she hadn't told any of them what had happened. 'Cause, what would they think? They wouldn't understand. They didn't have the capacity in their little brains for the subtleties of the situation. They'd come to a consensus around whatever simple answer came easiest, one that painted me as a monster, a trenchcoat mafia kind of guy, with no friends and no ideals and a heart full of hate, which isn't true. My heart's full of love. Everything I've ever done wrong or right in this world has been to protect the people I love.

ASHELEY

I kept waiting for Will or Craig—or both of them—to stumble in. Every time the front door opened, or the sliding door out back swooshed, I jumped a little. But I couldn't show it.

Smile, nod, fake it, pray. That was my mantra throughout the rest of the night.

It took me forever to get everyone out, and the whole time, I kept thinking, they can see through me, they can see the panic spazzing under my smile. Eventually, it was just me and Luke Pfifer—the fast-talking, aviator glasses–wearing runt who somehow had it in his head that he was a superstar—and his two dumpy hangers on, Toby Smith and Ricky Thomson. God knows how they even found out about the party, but they'd showed up early and made a beeline for the Wii. By now it was almost four in the morning and they were still taking turns beating each other's boxing Mii to a pulp. They didn't care what was going on around them. They were chortling and flailing and making cat calls at each other in the stupid made-up language they used, and it was pretty obvious they were never going to leave so I walked right over and turned the machine off. I didn't care. It was just Luke Pfifer.

"See ya, bye," I said. "Party's over."

Finally, once I got them out the door, I collapsed on the couch and let the events of the evening soak in. My eyes trailed up the shiny blond wooden railing that twisted around the edges of the room, following the stairs up along the various levels of platform. I'd been doing this for I don't know how many years, since I was born practically. But now the room seemed different. Less filled with air.

I panicked. The questions went flying through my head. Where were they? What was that text Will had sent supposed to have meant? What happened to Craig? Why hadn't he texted me too? And now this silence. It was all too much. Something bad, something so, so, so bad must have gone down.

My mouth started to water and I could feel the acid building in the back of my throat.

I leapt off the couch and raced out of the house.

There, on the porch, I gulped down the piney air and willed my body to stop rebelling against me. It was quiet except for the low hum of crickets. The yard was empty, dark in the weak light bleeding out from the living room.

"Will?" I called, in a hoarse whisper. "Are you there?"

Nothing.

There was a nip in the air. I was shivering. I waited for a

couple of seconds more, and then, just as I was going to step back inside to grab a sweatshirt, I heard a scratching, burrowing sound behind the shed.

I waited. I rubbed at my arms to warm them up. Still nothing. Must be a raccoon or a possum, I figured.

But I gave it a minute just to make sure.

The sound came back. Something moved back there. And a shadow started to emerge from the dark, person sized, moving slowly, timidly, into the light.

Will. I recognized his walk, the slight looseness at his elbows every time they swing. He was holding a golf club, resting it on his shoulder. As he came closer, his features started to take shape and then he was fully there, at the edge of the light, and that's when I saw the blood smeared across his face. He looked like a ghoul. Like one of those creepy guys he was always drawing.

I lost it. Completely. I can't say for sure if I understood yet what had happened. I was freaking out. I wasn't thinking anything. Just fear. That's all I was. Screams. Arms and legs shaking and shooting all over the place like there was something sick, something revolting, stuck to my skin and I had to get it off.

Then he was wrapped around me, pinning my arms to my sides and holding tight. Riding me out until I stopped bucking and heaving and kicking at him, until I gave up. I didn't exactly hug him back, but I let him contain me. I didn't have much choice, no way was he going to let me go. My muscles relaxed. I slid to the ground and he slid down with me, and when I leaned my weight into him, I could feel his chest heaving under me. He was crying too. There we were again, knotted together, both of us heaving and bawling our eyes out.

"What happened?" I whispered, once I could talk again. "Did—"

He clung to me tighter. For a second he stopped breathing. Then he let out this howl like something I'd never heard before, like an animal in such excruciating pain that it engulfs and swallows up the whole world. It was harrowing, that sound. I'll never forget it.

And then, it was like . . . I don't know . . .

I shuddered. There was, like, a flash, an image flaming through my mind. Of Craig, of . . . There was this sudden surge of emotion, like firecrackers going off in my chest and I shoved Will away from me. I kicked at him. "No. Get away from me. No. No," I said. I scooted backward across the lawn until I was out of his reach. I didn't want him to touch me.

And he just took it. He just sat there, crying, letting me kick him and whatever.

I stared at him. I hated him in that moment. But at the same time, I felt like, I don't know . . . It just . . . I was confused. I don't know. I don't know what I thought.

Slowly, shyly, he sat back, Indian style. "Ash," he said. "Something—"

"Shut up . . . Shut up, shut up!" I said. I didn't want to hear it. Like, if he didn't say it out loud, it wouldn't be real.

He laid back and we both sort of hung out there for a long time. I don't know how long. Will was staring up at the moon. It was huge, not quite a full moon, but a couple days off one. "That's a surfer moon," he said. "That moon means the waves are especially big. What if . . . What if he was surfing?" He fell into thought. "Night surfing. Alone. And . . . Craig could have—"

At the sound of Craig's name, I freaked out again. "Fuck you!" I shouted. "Don't say it. You don't deserve to say his name."

Will nodded. He rose to his feet and headed toward the shed. Then he stopped. "I'll need your help," he said, really quietly.

And I don't know. I didn't respond. It's not like I said, sure, whatever you need. I just kept staring at him. Then I wandered away, I remember wandering away. Somehow I ended up back in the house, wearing my Stanford sweatshirt. My comfort sweatshirt. I don't even remember putting it on. Thinking . . . I don't know what I was thinking.

I'd always trusted Will. I knew he wouldn't hurt me . . . he wouldn't hurt someone I loved. And . . . I guess I decided it must have been an accident. I couldn't believe he would have done it on purpose.

In the last few seconds out in the ditch, Craig had been thrashing and wrestling on top of me. He'd been pinning me down. It had hurt. Maybe. I don't know. I'd been scared. And then when Will had shown up . . . I mean, what would have happened if Will *hadn't* shown up? What would Craig have done? He'd been trying to protect me.

I went back outside. Will had dug one of Keith's old wet-suits out of the shed and laid it out like a body on the lawn—it was old, out of date, maybe from way back in the nineties. Keith had gone through at least two since then. He wouldn't miss it. He probably didn't even remember he had it.

I got the bike from the side of the road and I carted it with me as I followed Will along the path through the woods until we came to the fork where it veers off toward the cliffs.

And there he was. Lying there. Not moving. It . . . there was so much blood pooling around his head. He almost didn't look like a person anymore. I could feel the vomit edging up the back of my throat. And . . . it was all just too much. I think I just shut down, closed my emotions off completely. It was the only way I could handle it right then.

We didn't say a word. Neither of us. It would have been too much to talk. It would have made what we were doing real and I couldn't bear to face the idea that this could be anything more than an eerie nightmare, a movie we'd fallen into. Something I wasn't really taking part in.

I wasn't really thinking. My brain was black, totally shut off. Will would give me a direction, and like a zombie, I'd do what he said. I held the wetsuit open. It was all I could bring myself to do, and I kept my eyes shut the whole time. I didn't want to see it. I kept telling myself, this isn't Craig. This is something else, something like Craig but not.

Will handled the body, stuffing and adjusting it inside the wetsuit until everything was situated right and he could zip it up. Then he started dragging it by the collar toward the cliffs. I trailed after him, loitering, trying not to keep up.

When I got to the clearing, Will was sitting on a boulder holding his head in his hands—not just any boulder, actually, but his special rock. The one he goes to when he needs to think about his life. Craig's body was slumped on the ground below him.

"I need your help," he said. "I'm sorry. I can't do this part without you."

So, I . . . yeah. I *did* help him. It's not like I made a decision about it, I—I didn't have a choice. That's what it seemed like.

I took Craig's feet and Will took his arms and we swung him back and forth, picking up velocity, and finally let him go flying into the bay.

Then I waited there, shivering, even though it wasn't cold, while Will walked the bike down the path back to our yard and hid it in the shed out back.

And when he got back, we just stood there, for what seemed like forever, staring out across the water.

"Here's what we're going to say," Will told me. "He called you last night during the party to say he was going out for a midnight surf. Okay? You were against it. But he didn't care. He was drunk, slurring, all that. And if you wouldn't come watch him, he didn't care, he was going to go alone. We'll put that idea into the air, just as a quiet rumor. Then if his body washes up, it'll click for people. He wracked himself over the rocks out there. It'll all make sense. People won't think twice. Think you can do that?"

I think I maybe nodded. I was numb. I was only half hearing him.

"Okay," he said. He squeezed my hand. Then he climbed down to check things out.

I waited for him up top. I couldn't have moved if I'd wanted to. It was almost morning. Streaks of pink and yellow and purple were creeping across the sky. Like it had gotten its ass kicked during the night and now the wounds were beginning to show up. It looked like I felt. And I was pretty sure I'd be feeling that way nonstop for the rest of my life.

WILL

Sure, of course. There were a few scares. People talk, all the time, making up whatever craziness they want, and it's not like you can control their every thought. It's just gossip though. It's not real. It's not *actionable*. But it can get in your head. Just knowing people *might* be whispering can make things pretty hairy if you don't know how to keep your cool.

Like, for instance, I went golfing later that week. Tuesday. My usual. Keeping to the pattern. I went out alone and shot nine rounds and then stopped by the clubhouse for a lemonade before heading out to polish off the back nine. It was maybe twelve thirty, one. Right around then. And who was there, slurping on Diet Coke at the bar? Naomi.

I mean, it wasn't that unusual to see Naomi there. She's friendly with Sylvia, the hippie chick—well, ex-hippie chick, she's like fifty now—who's been working dayshifts there since God knows when. She babysits Sylvia's kids sometimes, I think.

Anyway, she was slouched over the countertop of the bar, chatting in a lazy way with Sylvia. The TV above the bar was tuned to some sort of Lifetime channel movie, and they were glancing at that a little bit too.

When I walked in, they both suddenly went completely silent. Naomi perked up. She swiveled to face me, bracing her back on the bar with her elbows in a way that sort of pushed her breasts out. On purpose? It seemed like it to me.

"Hey, killer party, Will," she said. She half smiled and took a long drag off her Diet Coke. "And your house—amazing. It's like a giant playpen. Like a dance club or something. Asheley says your dad made it."

It was awkward. Like she'd been rehearsing, thinking up small talk so she'd have something to say when I showed up. And I had no idea if this was because she was into me or because she was suspicious.

"Yeah, I guess that's true," I said.

"He must have been amazingly talented," she said.

What was I supposed to say to that? Tell her what an asshole he was? That would have seemed crazy.

She watched me really closely while I ordered my lemonade, freakily so, like she was trying to peer under my skin somehow, and I would have left right then, but you're not allowed to take the glasses out of the clubhouse, so I took a stool and tried to drink up.

"Hey, where'd you disappear to, anyway? You said you'd be right back and then I never saw you again. It's too bad. I was having fun talking to you." She paused dramatically, leaned over to bump my arm with her elbow, arched her eyebrow. "I spent like an hour looking for you, but—"

"You went looking for me? Where?"

"Oh, just around the house. I saw your room."

"You went in my room?"

"Sure. And I have to say, whoa, dude, what do you do in there? That place is so clean it's like you don't even live there. I thought guys' rooms were supposed to be bomb sites."

I had to keep reminding myself not to read anything into what she was saying. That if she'd seen anything, or was suspicious in any way, no way would she be acting so flirty.

"I mean, I didn't stay long," she said, "just sort of popped in and out."

"But why?"

"I don't know, Will. It was a party. I wanted to find you. Ask Sylvia, I'm totally shy. And I just, you know, every guy I've dated in the past year or so is just such a party boy. You seem like somebody I might be able to actually have a conversation with. Like we used to, back in Mrs. Kelley's class."

I was embarrassed. Relieved, 'cause if she was saying something like this, she must have no clue about what happened with Craig, but also, I don't know, freaked out because I didn't want her having a crush on me. I didn't want her rooting around in my life.

I glanced at Sylvia, who was pretending to be caught up in the Lifetime movie, and she gave me a shrug that seemed to be saying, hey, whatever life throws at you, gobble it up.

"We were, like, eleven when we were in Mrs. Kelley's class," I said.

Naomi must have got embarrassed then, too. She began futzing with her soda glass and glancing around for something to take her focus off of me. The next thing I knew, she was changing the subject. "Hey, so, Craig and Asheley," she said. "What's up with that?"

The heat rushed through me like I'd suddenly been thrown into a volcano. This had all been a setup. She knows. She knows. That's what went flashing through my mind. She was buttering me up and now she's pulling out the knives.

"With what," I sputtered. "What do you mean?"

"Uh, Claudia Jackson? He was playing grabass with her last week at Becca's? Don't tell me you didn't know. Everybody knows. They were right there in the pool, in front of everyone. Think Ash will forgive him?"

Bam! I was pulled out of the volcano and shoved headfirst into a tub of ice cubes. I was suddenly freezing, breaking apart. "Oh, that," I said. "Yeah, I don't know. You think she should?"

"I would. He's completely in love with her. From what I hear, he's a total wreck about the whole thing. I mean, like not bathing, not leaving the house torn up over her."

And then the weirdest thing occurred. I was suddenly fine. Suave. Savvy. I was suddenly someone who wasn't me at all. I was a new Will, a better Will, in absolute control of my situation. I saw my opening and I leapt right in. "Yeah, I heard that too," I said. "Word on the street is he's so upset that he's fled town."

"You're kidding."

"That's what I heard. I mean, not from Asheley, she won't even let me mention his name, but from, I don't know, around. He's run off to Palm Springs to hang with his grandparents, or something like that."

"Jesus. That's too bad."

"Right?" I touched her arm, lightly flicked my finger back and forth over her skin. I realized that this meant I was invading her space, but I didn't care. It was mine to invade. It seemed, at that moment, that I could do whatever I wanted and no one would stop me. If I wanted to kiss her, I could have kissed her. "But hey," I said. "At least I'm still here."

Glancing at my hand on her elbow, she said, "Very true. And I'm still here."

"You are."

I flicked my finger across her skin again, this time with more urgent intent, and she picked my hand up and set it down on the bar, putting a few inches of space between us. But she was grinning. She wasn't rejecting me.

"Maybe we could hang out sometime," she said.

"Yeah, maybe."

"Like, sometime soon?"

"You know my mom's out of town until, like, August," I said.

There was some sort of ache pulsing inside her so strongly that I could see it surging toward me. So, that's what desire looks like, I thought. I'd never known it was so easy to see. But I didn't make a move. I'd done enough damage. What I did instead was down my lemonade, touch her arm again, briefly, and leave her hanging.

It wasn't until I was outside dragging my golf bag toward the tenth tee that I realized I'd given her an open invitation to stop by the house anytime she felt like it.

Jesus, I thought. That's gonna be trouble.

ASHELEY

I was spooked. No matter how hard I tried to not think about it, those hours out in the dark with Will kept coming back, repeating themselves in slow motion in my mind. Every time I closed my eyes, I'd get a flash of Craig's body crumpled on the ground, stuffed like trash into that wetsuit. And I'd ache. There'd be a tingling at the edges of my heart, urging me to take action, to stop Craig from dying, but I couldn't—how could I? He was already dead.

Every second of every day seemed like it would be the one when we would get caught.

What I did is I sort of hid out. I stopped going to softball practice. I didn't return texts from Naomi or anybody else. I barely made it to work most days, sort of racing there just under the gun, punching in, and then zombieing out for eight hours until it was time to leave.

I took these long meandering walks, just going, just moving through the fresh air. They helped a little. Three or four hours of walking like that and I almost felt close to human sometimes.

On one of these walks, I ran into a bunch of my softball girls. Or not exactly ran into. They were sunbathing on the rocky shoreline, those long slabs of black rock that emerge during low tide down around the bend from the state park and I saw them from a ways off as I was coming up from the beach. Ruth, Crystal, Becca and Naomi. They were laying out in their bikinis, watching the sailboats and jet skis skim around in the bay, and they had all sorts of gear with them—sunscreen, plush beach blankets, a cooler full of Diet Coke, a mondo bag of Pirate's Booty, magazines, a ball and a couple of mitts.

For a while there, I didn't get too close. I was nervous about seeing them—and I was jealous. They looked so relaxed, so summery. Perfect, really. Like they *were* summer—bright and warm and lazy and without a single worry in the world. All the things I'd never be able to be again, if I'd ever been able to be like that.

But I couldn't stop myself from creeping closer. I still really wanted to be accepted as part of the group. I hugged the edge of the tree, not really hiding, but not going out of my way to be obvious. If one of them saw me, I'd just wave, I figured, and they'd think I just arrived. I mean, I was already wearing my baby-blue one-piece and a tie-dye wrap. If you didn't notice the cloud over my head, you'd think I fit right in. Nobody'd know I'd been spying on them.

They were talking about boys. Big surprise. Just gossiping, who's into who, who's not so into who, that sort of thing. Turned out Ruth had hooked up with Lewis from the golf team at my party. That was news to me. She'd talked to him twice since then, and he'd been saying all the right things, how he'd been wanting to get close to her for months, how cool it would be if she wanted to stop over one afternoon while his parents were at work and hang out by his pool, all that, but she wasn't sure she wanted to get too close. She didn't trust him. "Those guys on the golf team, they're all sort of pricks," she said.

"Not all of them," said Naomi. "There's Will."

Just hearing his name come up in their conversation sent a spike of dread running down my back.

"Okay, sure, Will's not a prick," said Ruth, "but he's a freak. You know?"

"He's not like he used to be," said Naomi. She pulled her sunglasses down from the place where they were lodged in her hair and covered her eyes with them.

"No? Why?" Ruth said. "You can be a jock and still secretly be a freak. Uh, Tiger Woods, anyone?"

"He's fine," Naomi said. "He's just a little weird." If she was trying to defend him, she wasn't doing much of a job of it.

"Yeah, but he still gets that look on his face sometimes," said Becca. "You know the one I mean? Like he's either about to start bawling or pull out some nunchucks and do some sort of insane ninja job on you."

"It's true," Ruth said. She just wouldn't give it up. "You can douse your face with Noxzema, you can buy some new clothes and start brushing your hair, but does that really change anything? I mean, does that make you any less of a serial killer?"

"I wouldn't say he's a serial killer," Naomi mumbled.

"Okay, maybe a child molester. Did you see him at the party Saturday? There were a couple moments when I was almost scared."

Even Becca got in on the action. "Remember freshman year when Reed Calhoon stole his comic book in study hall and he screamed so loud you could hear it all the way over in the gym? Weird Willy Wanker!"

They broke out laughing—all of them, even Naomi cracked a little grin.

"Weird Willy Wanker," the words bubbled out of Crystal's mouth between laughs. "I'd forgotten all about that one."

Ruth's face tightened into a vindictive smile. She threw a cruel glance at Naomi. "Weird. Willy. Wanker," she said, like each word was boulder she was throwing into the ocean. "Is he a good kisser, Naomi?"

Naomi's face went red. "What? No! How would I know?"

"I saw you flirting with him at that party."

For a moment, Naomi looked like she was going to vomit up all the Pirate's Booty she'd been scarfing down, then she swallowed real slowly and said, "For like, two seconds, maybe, yeah, but then he totally disappeared. Like ran away scared . . ." She trailed off and pulled her knees tighter toward herself like she was suddenly embarrassed and confused.

Thinking that if they saw me, maybe they'd feel a touch of collective shame, I moved out from the tree line and picked my way across the rocks toward them.

They'd stopped talking, briefly. Naomi was digging in her beach bag for something. Ruth was looking triumphant, her chin held a little too high as she gazed out across the water. Crystal had grabbed the bag of Pirate's Booty and was throwing puffs one at a time into the air trying to catch them with her teeth.

The first one to see me was Becca. She didn't even flinch. "Asheley!" she said. "We were just talking about your party."

This caught me off guard. I almost tripped over a crack in the rock I was standing on. They all looked up at once.

"Hey, where was Craig," asked Ruth. "Hard to believe he wouldn't have shown up." She was scrutinizing me, holding her glasses up away from her eyes, and for a second I was sure she had seen him, that she knew what had happened and was holding on to this information until she could use it to do the most damage. "Don't tell me you dumped him over Claudia Jackson."

Oh. It was just that. More soap opera.

I sputtered, trying to think of what to say. "I, uh, I haven't really seen him. I . . . it's been rocky. I don't know, I . . ."

Naomi looked up from her bag. "He went to Palm Springs." She said this so matter-of-factly that there was no way of arguing with it. Like it was a fact, no question. "That's what I heard. He's at his grandmother's house, trying to figure out how to get over you. When he gets back, though, Ash, you should forgive him. Really."

So, wow. Where'd she hear that? I didn't know what to think. First she trash-talks Will, then she comes up with this crazy stuff about Craig leaving town. Whose side was she on? Or did she even know herself?

"Maybe I will," I told her. "I've been missing him." Which was totally true.

Then I jetted out of there before any of them could see me cry.

WILL

We were in a school bus. Mom, Dad, me, and Asheley. Dad was driving, he was singing and driving—you are my sunshine, my only sunshine—driving real slow up the Pacific Coast High-way, and the rest of us were sitting way in the back row. There were duffel bags and boxes of food and stuff stacked up in the rows in front of us. We were headed to Big Sur, I knew this, I don't know why, and everyone was chatty and excited about it. I'd done the packing and I was feeling real proud of what a good job I'd done, holding the checklist Dad had made for me and reading it over and over again: sleeping bags, check; flashlights, check; Coleman lamp, check; all these necessities, check, check, check, check, and I remember thinking, *this is why Dad's happy, because I checked off everything on the list.* And then somehow we discovered that a bunch of the rows near the front of the bus had been taken out so there was a big open space there, and Ash said, "Let's put up the tent! We can be camping now!" So I opened the sleeve and dumped everything out and it turned out there weren't any tent poles. "Don't tell your dad," Mom whispered and Dad stopped singing. "What's that?" he said. And 'cause Ash was so little and easily excited, she toddled up to the driver's seat and said, "We forgot the tent poles!" She sort of sang it.

Screech. Dad pulled off the side of the road and came racing back toward us, shouting at Mom, "Deb, what did I tell you? What about the list? You just check things off on the list. It's not rocket science." And then he's dragging her by the collar of her T-shirt, ripping it, she's bucking and pulling behind him, down the steps and out the door. Asheley's screaming and I'm watching them argue, my face and hands pressed to the window. They're on this lip of black rock, like a thousand feet up, but I know there's ocean down there, I can hear it roaring. And then, somehow, the tent's out there too, flapping around in Dad's other hand, and he kicks Mom's legs out from under her and straddles her and pulls the tent tight between his fists and he's got it stretched across her face. He's suffocating her. "Will!" she says. "Will!" And I can't tell if she's begging me to help her or if she's telling Dad that this is all my fault. Either way, he's up and off her now and coming toward me, snapping the tent like a whip as he comes, stomping up the steps and down the aisle until he's right there on top of me, his face huge and full of rage and the tent comes up between us and I can't see, all of a sudden I can't see, it's just gray and pink plastic everywhere, but weirdly not violent at all, sort of soft and tender and I hear myself shout and then I hear Asheley.

"Hey. Hey. It's okay, Will. It's not real."

I opened my eyes and she was peering over me, smoothing my hair down, coaxing me back.

"It sort of is real," I said to her. "Dad used to . . ." But then, I stopped myself. I couldn't tell her about all the crap Dad used to pull. I mean, what would that gain me? It would shatter her, and she probably wouldn't have believed me anyway.

ASHELEY

Those nightmares, my God. They were just nonstop. He never told me what happened in them. "Bad memories," he'd say. They were horrible, though. He'd be whimpering, gasping, then I'd hear him scream bloody murder and I'd go running in to calm him down.

The only thing that seemed to help was if I held him, rocked him like a baby, until he fell asleep.

And then, of course, I'd fall asleep too, half the time, there on his bed. He was a total wreck. As torn up about what had happened with Craig as I was. I mean, we took care of each other. I was really trying to help him hold it together.

WILL

Even with Asheley there, I'd shudder awake every couple hours or so and lay in the dark with my eyes wide open, staring at the keepsakes all carefully organized in my room. It's like all that stuff, I'd used it to remind myself who I was, and now it belonged to someone else. The Phil Mickelson posters and the framed photos of me as a kid, grinning, swinging my clubs, so proud, the comic books, wrapped in Mylar and stacked in their box, all of it, even the trophy I'd won, what, three weeks ago— it wasn't me anymore. I'd become someone else and I had no idea who that someone else was.

On the shelf above my desk, I've got this Mexican Day of the Dead figurine, just a cheap thing, it's made of paper that's been dipped in wax. It's like a farmer or something, a skeleton man wearing a poncho and a huge sombrero, carrying a crate full of hot peppers. And he's laughing. His head is a skull. He's got these glowing yellow eyes. And his jaw sort of hangs open in this crazy grin. And I'd lay awake there, staring at him, staring at his open mouth and, just, think about crawling up inside and shivering there.

Thinking.

And Ash, since the thing with Craig, she'd been sort of shell-shocked. She'd had a hard time being alone, so she was sleeping in my room sometimes. She'd be sprawled out next to me, her legs kicked in all sorts of angles, her mouth open just a soft fraction, making these quiet noises, like she was purring or something. Once in a while, she'd rub at her nose with the palm of her hand and gum her lips a couple times—all this while still asleep—and it was . . . you know? It was the most precious thing I think I've ever seen. She moved around a lot in her sleep, and eventually she'd have the covers balled around her, scooched all the way over to my side of the bed and I'd be hanging there on the edge, trying to make myself as thin as I possibly could so that I didn't touch her, so I wouldn't disturb her or give her the wrong impression.

It was calming, having her there. I'd wake up at noon and realize I'd somehow managed to nod off after all.

I know this isn't what you asked me about. It's all related, though. For the other stuff to make sense, I need to explain this too. I'm not sure why. Should I keep going?

Okay, so there was one morning when Ash was sleeping in my bed and I was jolted awake by noises in the kitchen. Something was rooting around down there. My first thought was, cops. That got me up and out of bed. But these noises, they

weren't brutal, they weren't the sounds of someone searching and ransacking, they were calm, organized. They had the
rhythm of familiarity. Anyway, it was, like, seven in the morning and I figured if they were going to come arrest me, they'd
shoot to do it with an eye on it making the evening news.

It was Keith, of course. I peered over the railing and caught
a glance at him, straightening things in the living room.

Right away, I shut my door tight, letting Asheley sleep, and
shuffled down the platforms toward the ground level. Quietly. It was important not to let him know I was awake until I
was down there. I didn't want him poking around and catching sight of her curled up in my bed. When I got to her level,
I peeked in to see what kind of state her room was in. The covers were bunched between the bed and the wall. It was obvious
she'd been sleeping there at some point the night before.

I pulled her door tight, hoping it wasn't too late. I just
knew Keith's mind would slide to the sleaziest conclusions
if he found out she was in my room. It always does. It would
be inconceivable to him that we'd just been sleeping. He'd be
imagining all the things *he'd* do to her if he had her alone in a
bed all night long.

Then I continued down the stairs, and tying my flannel
pajama bottoms at the waist, I plopped myself down on the
second-to-last rung where the stair-platforms jut into the open
space between the kitchen and living room areas.

By now Keith had made his way into the kitchen. He had
the dishwasher open and was collecting glasses and stacking
them in the tray.

"What is this, maid service?" I asked him.

He was dressed for hiking—a pair of faded cargo shorts and his work boots laced up tight, a thick blue work shirt open over one of his hundreds of worn-out T-shirts.

"Just checking in," he said.

"I told you, you didn't have to do that."

"Yeah, but see, you're seventeen. I'm fifty-three."

"What does that have to do with anything?"

"That means I'm a little better at knowing what has to be done than you are."

I made a *humpfing* sound, and stopped myself from saying the smart-ass remark that came to my mind hearing this crap from him. It wasn't a good idea to push it that morning. Best to be civil and get rid of him quickly.

"How long have you been here?"

"Oh, half an hour, maybe. I needed my work gloves. I've got a job for a few days helping this guy in Larkspur put in a new deck."

Work gloves. That meant he'd been rooting around in the shed. Where I'd hidden the bike. I had to know if he'd seen it. I couldn't ask, but I had to know.

"You don't even have to come in the house to get your gloves. You can just walk around to the shed and—"

"Got 'em." He dug a pair of stiff yellow leather gloves out the cargo pocket of his shorts. "Then I figured, why not throw you guys a party? Bacon and eggs. See how it's hanging."

He stopped what he was doing then, and holding a coffee mug over the dishwasher, gave me a look that might have been saying, *I know something weird's going on, Will*. Hard to tell. You can't really read much in his facial expressions because of those giant plastic glasses of his.

"So," he said. "How's it hanging?"

"I don't see any bacon and eggs."

"Yeah, well." He motioned toward the piles of dirty dishes strewn all over the countertops. "First things first, hey?"

I sat there and watched him work, waiting for him to ask about the bike. Craig's bike. I'd hidden it in the shed. I could come up with an excuse, that wasn't the problem, the problem was that if enough little clues popped up, the lies might start to contradict each other.

He didn't ask about the bike, though. Instead, as he poured the detergent in and turned on the dishwasher, he said, "So, bacon and eggs?"

"Sure," I said. "Whatever. Hey, don't you have to be at that job?"

"Eight thirty. I've got time. Not to eat, but to cook up a meal for you, anyway."

I nodded my consent.

"Scrambled? With garlic and cheddar, that's how you like 'em, yeah?"

"Yeah."

"Okay, then. Bacon and scrambled eggs for one, coming right up." Keith is even more aggravating when he's trying to be all folksy and dad-like. "Hey, where's Asheley, anyway?" he said.

So, it was going to come after all. "What do you mean?" I said.

"She's not here."

"How do you know?"

"I checked on her, man."

"Did you check on me too?"

"Naw. Your door was shut. Anyway, Asheley's my girl, you know? I check on you and you might pull a gun on me."

"Good one."

"So, what, is she off getting some nookie with that surfer dude of hers?"

He was hovering over the pan, dropping bacon strips into it. His back was turned to me. I had to just assume and pray he wasn't fishing.

"Yeah, that's it," I said.

He wheezed. "I would be too."

"Craig. His name's Craig. And she's not off getting 'nookie' with him. She's at her friend Naomi's house," I said. That was safe. There'd be no checking up. Keith didn't know Naomi. "They're having a sleepover."

"That's what she said," Keith said in his best Steve Carell imitation, then he glanced at me and grinned. "She's getting nookie."

"Whatever, man. Ash is a good girl," I muttered.

And that was it. He made the eggs, he left. I sat there trying to figure out if I was hungry or not.

It was good to have him gone.

And also, I'd surprised myself a little. I'd played it pretty cool. It seemed like, maybe, I was getting better at this not freaking out every two seconds thing.

What I really wanted to do was to shuffle back upstairs and

cuddle up in bed with Asheley. To slide my arm around her waist and spoon her. Just snuggle all morning, maybe doze off again. But, I don't know, that seemed dangerous to me. Too much, too soon, or something. It seemed icky.

Like I said, I didn't want her to get the wrong impression.

ASHELEY

On Friday night, Naomi showed up unannounced at the house. She had the waistband of her sweats provocatively rolled down, her hair clipped up out of her lightly made-up face, her everything just so carefully planned to look casual and accidentally sexy.

I almost teared up when I opened the door and saw it was her. It was just so nice to see someone besides Will.

She gave me a silly, sort of coy little wave, and peering over my shoulder, shouted across the house to Will. "Hey there, superstar. I made it!"

All afternoon, Will and I had been playing *Halo*—or Will had been, anyway, trash-talking into his headset and racing around that eerie, glowing, bombed-out world, stalking his opponent—some kid from Thailand, I think—killing him over and over and over again. It relaxed him. I'd been curled up on the couch watching him. As long as it was just the two of us all alone in the house, I could almost convince myself that the fear was gone, that we were normal again and everything was going to be fine now.

And now, with Naomi stopping by, I wondered if maybe the worst really was over, if now things really were going to be normal again.

Will leaned back, still playing the game, and looked upside down toward the door. Seeing it was Naomi, he gave her a wave.

"Took you long enough," he said.

"Better late than never, yeah?"

She dropped her oversized silver shoulder bag on the floor and plopped herself down next to him on the couch.

"Hey," she said, rapping Will on the shoulder with the back of her fingers.

"Hey," he said. It was weird—and sort of sad—to see him blush. I had to keep shoving back the urge to protect him.

He went on playing the game, and for a while we watched him, awkwardly catching up. She kept asking about Craig. Like, "Is he back yet? You're totally going to try and work it out, right? Have you heard from him? I bet he's back and just afraid to call. You sure you haven't heard from him? You must miss him horribly. I know I would. Hey, what if you were to go over to his house right now, show up and surprise him, what do you think he'd do? Will, don't you think that's a good idea?"

"No," he said. Just like that. Blunt and direct. He didn't even glance away from his game.

"Hey, can we, like, talk about something else," I said.

"It's too painful, right?" Naomi said. She slid off the couch and scooched up close to Will. "Still, you're going to have to see him sometime. If you want to work it out with him, I mean."

Will shot me a lunatic, terrified look.

Then finally, I got it. I felt like a dunce. She was there on a mission. This was a booty call. Will had a booty call! Wow! That was a first! And me hanging around was messing it all up.

But it's not like I could leave. That would have been totally obvious. And where would I have gone? All this talking about Craig was making my heart ache. The thought of leaving the safety of my house was just too much to bear.

Will zapped off the game and jumped up to his feet. "Who's thirsty," he said. "We've still got three quarters of a bottle of tequila left from those margaritas. What do you guys say? Shots?" The way he was nodding at me made it clear, he wanted me to stay, and if I did, he'd do his best to be entertaining, steering the conversation away from Craig. If we acted like everything was completely normal, we might, for a while, convince ourselves it was.

"You have limes? And salt?" asked Naomi.

"You better believe it."

"I'm in then," she said.

"Sure. I'm in too," I said.

Will ran to the kitchen and grabbed the tequila and everything else he needed, then brought it all back to the coffee table. The only shot glasses he could find were these corny, flowery Betty Boop ones that Mom collected, and as we downed our first round, I couldn't help thinking, Jesus, is this how she started out? Downing shots to avoid how uncomfortable she felt? I said a little prayer not to turn out like her.

But, you know, liquor has a way of tricking you out of whatever crazy emotions you're feeling and dunking you into even crazier situations.

For the second round, Naomi decided that we should do body shots. Instead of licking the salt on our own wrists, we'd lick it off of someone else's neck. She went first, and of course, she chose Will, coming in long and slow, and sort of lingering on his skin just a second too long.

When she pulled away from Will, she stuck her tongue out at me and said, "I'm sorry about the other day at the beach, Ash."

"What are you talking about?" I asked, even though I knew exactly what she was talking about.

"I know you heard what everybody was saying," she said. "I mean, obviously. But screw them, you know? Catty bitches. They were really sort of pissing me off, actually."

This was nice to hear. I'd always suspected that Naomi was more sensitive than the average girl in our town, that she'd be a loyal friend if we were given a chance. "Thanks," I said. "I mean, you have no idea how much I appreciate that."

"What are you two talking about?" asked Will, flashing me a look, thinking, I could tell, that maybe we weren't as safe as we thought we were.

"Nothing," I said. "Everything's *fine*."

"Your turn!" shouted Naomi, wrapping her arm around Will's shoulder. "Body shot!"

He hesitated, glancing at me for assurance, then took a

quick body shot off her neck, barely touching her, squirming almost, he was so uncomfortable. Poor Will. He had no idea how to be sensual, and now that I thought about it, I understood that Naomi really did like him, she wasn't just playing. How nice would it be for him to know what it felt like to have someone touch him, someone who wanted him, who couldn't get enough of him? And in that case, why *not* Naomi?

"Here. Will. This is how it's done," I said. I licked Naomi's neck and sprinkled salt on it. Then I shot my tequila, and leaned in to suck the salt off of her skin, making sure to use a lot of lip and tongue, to be as sensual as I could about the whole thing.

Will paid close attention, but I'm not sure he got my point.

Anyway, after that, things got pretty crazy. We kept doing shots and eventually we somehow ended up playing Truth or Dare.

It wasn't until a few questions in, when Naomi asked me, "What would you say to Craig if he walked in here right now and begged you to come back to him?" that I realized how close to danger we were playing with this game. I downed another shot. Somehow the fact that the game demanded I not lie made it harder for me to swat the question away. "Uh," I said, "I guess, I'd be amazed. I don't know."

Will, seeing that I was on the verge of breaking down, leapt in. "My turn," he said. "Ash, truth or dare?"

"Dare." No way was I ever going to take truth again.

"I dare you . . . to sit on my lap."

I could do that. He was perched on the twisty white leather ottoman, and I balanced myself on his leg. He wrapped his hand around my waist and supported me. Naomi made an expression, like, *he's your brother, dude*, and I smiled coyly at her and said, "Naomi, truth or dare?"

"Dare."

"I dare you . . . to sit on Will's lap with me."

"I guess if you dared me, I have to, don't I," she said, standing up and sauntering toward us with her best sexy walk.

He gave me a little squeeze, and I squeezed him back. I was trying to make it clear, *go for it, don't let me stop you*. He was trying to communicate something to me with his eyes, wiggling his eyebrows, ticking his cheek, but I couldn't tell what exactly it was. I figured he was just nervous. Intimacy. It was all new to him.

Once she was seated there on his lap, Naomi raced right past go. She nuzzled up close and wrapped both arms around him. "I think I missed some salt there," she said, and she kissed him on the neck, kneading the muscles in his back with her fingers. The kiss kept on going, up toward his ear, then across his cheek, then finally, she was kissing him on the lips. Will was just frozen there, not exactly spitting her out, but not helping either. Just terrified. But I figured, he must be liking it, too.

Anyway, my work was done. Whatever came next would have to be between them. I pried Will's fingers off of my waist and slipped to the floor.

Will reared his head back to avoid Naomi's kisses. "Ash?" he said. His face was a mess of concern. He reached out toward me, but Naomi reeled him back in.

"What's the matter?" she whispered. "This is supposed to be *fun*."

"Yeah, Will," I said. "Relax, have some fun. She's not going to bite you."

But, God, was he awkward. He didn't have any idea where to put his hands. He'd try one place, then another, shoot me mystified looks. And Naomi, she was trying to help—she watched his hands, caught his eye, darted her head back and forth in search of direction, tried to anticipate and adjust to his movement. And all the while, they were whispering in each other's ears.

Eventually, Will seemed to loosen up. He didn't struggle so much, started going with the flow. Instead of being terrified, he smiled when she spoke to him, a sort of wincing smile, but still.

They'd gotten cozy enough that I felt like, maybe I should duck out, head to my room, give them some privacy. It pleased me to see them this way. Like, maybe despite all the horror we'd been through, there would be a future for us after all. I liked Naomi so much. I thought if Will let her get close to him, she might mellow him.

I stood up and stretched. "I'm exhausted," I said. Then heading for the stairs, I said, "Have fun, kids."

Will called out behind me, "Hey, wait, Ash, don't just leave me—"

And as I turned back to see what he wanted, I saw . . . I can't say precisely what it was I saw. Motion. Movement. Him rising up and Naomi tumbling forward, real fast.

Naomi let out a yelp as she went flying. Hands out in front of her. Her head pounded against the corner of the coffee table, and I raced toward her to see if she was okay.

Then I caught the red, angry expression on Will's face, and I thought, *oh God, what happened? What did I miss?*

And Naomi, once she recovered herself, started screaming about how we were sick, horrible people and I knew, I just knew that Will must have said something to her about Craig. I mean, he must have intimated somehow that Craig was . . . that . . .

This is really difficult.

Dead. That's what I'm trying to say. That Craig was dead.

I mean, the expression on her face. It was pure terror, not just of Will, but of me too. And she booked it out of there as fast as she could. Raced out the back door and out across the yard.

Will shot me a glance and went chasing after her and I, I don't know, I slumped to the couch and tried to hold my head in. My brain felt like it was exploding. Because, that look Naomi'd given me, so accusatory, like she thought I was as guilty as Will, and was I? I hoped not. I couldn't bear the thought that maybe I was.

You have to understand, I was messed up in my head. I didn't think twice about what he might be doing out there with her.

WILL

Yeah, she fell.

She lost her balance, and she fell.

I don't know what to tell you, that's what happened.

Well, okay, let's go back to when they were both sitting on my lap. I was on the ottoman. Each of them was on one of my knees. And then, Asheley slid away and I felt some sort of chill— not like I was physically cold, but more like a premonition of how desperately alone I was in the world, how dead my life was when she wasn't near me. And I reached out to try and pull her back. Maybe she doesn't understand this. It wasn't some immature fear of girls, it wasn't that I was shy, it was a specific, piercing need to have her, Asheley, near me. I mean, it wasn't sexual or anything, it was just . . . we're a team, you know?

My heart must have lurched. I must have tensed up or something.

Naomi shifted so she could face me. "What's that about?" she said. She rubbed my chest with the tips of her fingers.

Ash was sitting on the floor, watching us, like monitoring to make sure I was having fun. "Yeah, Will," she said. "Relax, have some fun. She's not going to bite you." She's innocent—she's always been innocent—and I could tell, her hopes for me made it hard for her to fathom the possibility that I might not be interested in Naomi. I mean, from her point of view, the fact that someone, anyone, wanted to be my girlfriend was thrilling. Especially if it was someone she liked as much as she liked Naomi.

So I tried. I wanted to please her. If it would make her happy to see me in a kind of compromising position with her friend, I figured, I'd do my best to oblige.

I bounced Naomi on my knee, wrapped both arms around her waist and tucked her in tight to me. "What's what about?" I asked her.

"Why are you so concerned with Asheley?"

We were whispering, I doubt Ash could hear us.

"I don't know. I'm not," I said.

I kissed her, then, and she whispered to me, "You better not be. That would just be sick."

"Well, you're what I'm concerned with right now." I played my fingers across the small of her back.

"Good," she said. "That's how I want it to be."

We started to make out.

And from the corner of my eye, I saw Ash stand up and

stretch. She yawned. "I'm exhausted," she said. "You kids have fun."

And she padded off toward the stairs, and I just, I panicked. I reached out toward her. "Ash, don't, no! There's room for you, too!" I said. I leapt up, not even thinking that Naomi might . . . It's not like I was trying to hurt her. She lost her balance. She went tumbling off my lap and her head ricocheted off the coffee table.

Naomi laid there, stunned, for a few seconds. And she was bleeding really badly from the cut on her forehead. Then she sat up and held her hands up to her head, like rocking herself, mumbling, "Oh my God, oh my God, oh my God."

Asheley ran to her to see if she was okay, but Naomi wouldn't let her near her. She shook her off, shrieking. "You guys are sick," she said. "Sick! Sick! Sick!"

She pulled herself to her feet and stumbled to the sliding glass door.

And I chased after her. I had to. I needed to talk to her, at least, to convince her she was wrong about what she thought.

She was in good shape, though. Quick. All that softball training. She got out the door and was down across the yard before I'd even made it to the porch. For a second there I couldn't find her. She'd disappeared.

I waited.

I listened.

A rustling behind the shed, and then she darted out into the light briefly, saw me, spun, and headed toward the woods.

"Naomi, wait," I shouted.

She paused and glanced back at me.

"What? What do you want with me?" she said. "Sorry I'm not Asheley, you pervert."

She took two steps toward me, then she glanced to the side, like into the open door of the shed. She'd done a full circle around it. She saw something there. Her back went up like a cat's.

Then she shrieked and raced down the trail into the woods.

What had made her scream like that? What had she seen? Then I remembered. Craig's bike. I'd stashed it there. It was up near the door. Its handlebars and that front wheel with the shielding inside it—that green-slime smiley face sticking out its tongue that everyone recognized as his—were . . . she must have seen it.

And so I chased after her. I'd been barefoot, and I kept stepping on twigs and stones and shit like that, losing my footing. Thinking the whole time, my God, I better catch her, I can't let her go telling everyone in town about what happened tonight, all the crazy things she thought were going on with Asheley and me—wrong, they were wrong, but still, who'd care about that?—about Craig's bike and all the questions that would bring up. I had to protect us. I had to protect Asheley. So I didn't care about how my feet got torn up. I picked up my speed, pushed as hard as I could.

She was getting away, darting through the trees, staying off the path. She took a leap over a downed tree trunk, and she must have caught her toe, because she went sailing head first toward the ground. She was stunned just long enough for me to catch up to her.

And then—well, you know what happened then.

Yeah. That's her in the second photo.

No! Don't show it to me again! I'm just telling you, that's her.

By the time I made it back to the house, I was exhausted. I didn't even think about cleaning up. Ash was still sitting on the living room floor, like frozen there. She hadn't moved a muscle all the time I'd been gone. She was staring at the smudge of blood Naomi had left on the hardwood floor, barely blinking.

When she heard the door slide shut, she looked up at me and just seemed so shattered, so vacant and numb.

I tried to comfort her, but when I got near her, she threw her arms up and flailed and said, "No. No no no. I need . . . to think. I need . . ."

"When you're ready," I said, backing up, "I'll be here."

I walked around behind her and sat on the floor—not too close—and I laid my palm steady on the small of her back, just so she knew I was there, so she'd understand I cared.

ASHELEY

After that, I felt like . . . I mean, I hadn't *done* anything. I didn't *kill* anybody. But . . . that look Naomi had on her face before she ran out of the house that night. If she'd thought I was guilty—and she was a friend of mine—and then immediately after her looking at me like that, Will had gone and—I mean, wouldn't everybody else think I was guilty too? And was I guilty? And if so, what would happen to me if I got caught?

So, I couldn't just freak out and be sad and all that, I had to worry about being caught. I had to, like, pretend I was somebody else, almost. But I *was* sad. And scared. And totally freaked out. So . . .

Like, for instance, maybe two days after that night with Naomi, I was at work and Luke Pfifer, Toby Smith, and Ricky

Thomson strolled in. They were snickering and whispering to themselves—that's nothing new; they're always snickering about something. Toby had a pair of World War II aviator's goggles perched on his forehead. He kept playing around with them, taking them off, putting them back on, and I figured the three of them must have been all hopped up about that. They like that sort of thing. The more obscure something is, the more likely they are to proclaim it to be the coolest thing in the world—especially if it's got some sort of war-related profile. In our town, with its total rich lefty vibe, loving the military and its noble history is just about as far out of the box as you can get.

When their turn came to order, though, as I scooped out their ice cream and put the sprinkles and marshmallow gunk and what all, they got serious all of a sudden. They stood up straighter. They scrutinized me like I was one of their science projects.

"Rough day, huh?" Luke said to me.

"Not particularly." I tried to pull a smile, something that had been almost impossible for me to do since the night Naomi had come to the house.

He made a face, a mixture of pity and self-satisfaction. "You're still in denial."

Toby jumped in. "That's the first stage of grief, babe. You've got a long way to go."

"I have no idea what you dudes are talking about," I said, shoving their cups of ice cream across the counter.

"You're kidding, right?" said Luke.

"I'm totally not kidding."

"Naomi?"

The blood started pulsing like hammers behind my ears. Just hearing her name spoken made me lose all my strength. But I kept it together enough to stay on my feet.

"Whoa," said Ricky. "She really doesn't know."

"You should sit down for this," said Luke.

He was right. I pulled the swivel stool, painted with black-and-white cow markings, up underneath me and leaned back on it. My mind was running through the possibilities, all the variations they might be about to spew, and what each might mean for me and my brother. "Get it over with, already, huh, guys?" I said, struggling to hold my voice steady.

"Okay, you know those rocks out by Monarch Grove where the hippie nudists like to hang out and get sunburns?" Luke had taken a wide dramatic stance, arms out in front of him, like he was going to act the whole thing out. "The ones, they're like fifteen feet out or so and they disappear underwater at high tide? So, this morning a bunch of them were sitting around down there, doing some sort of sunrise meditation ritual, and that obese one—you know who I mean? With the red hair and the Fu Manchu mustache?—he slipped and his foot shot into the water onto something squishy. So, okay, fine, that was weird. But then, like five minutes later, they're still doing their mediation, and something comes floating up from the spot where the guy fell. And what was it? Naomi! I'm not kidding you. She was wearing this men's wetsuit, like, way too big for her but her body had blown up to like twice its size, so it actually sort of fit, weirdly. And her head was smashed in like a crash test dummy. Totally nasty, right?" He waited, eyes bugging out, for my reaction.

"And sad," said Ricky.

"Yeah, and sad too. I didn't mean to say it wasn't sad," said Luke.

"You two used to hang out, right?" said Ricky.

I nodded. I wasn't sure what to say. They were expecting something, so I tried the first thing that made it through my head. "Just her? They didn't find . . ." I stopped myself, but not before opening up a whole mess of problems.

They caught my mistake, though. Of course they did. There's all kinds of crap you can say about those guys, but you can't say they're not smart. The twisted up expressions on their faces, the mutters—*What? Huh? What do you mean "just her"?*—I had to come up with an explanation fast.

And so, what did I do? I just started blabbing. "Nothing. It's just . . . it makes sense now in a sort of way," I said. "Saturday night I got this weird call from Craig. At like three in the morning. I mean, I didn't answer. I got it the next morning. But he was acting completely crazy on the message. Begging me, *pick up, pick up, pick up*, and crying about how couldn't take it anymore, how he was going to . . ." This was a hole I was digging for myself. I knew it. I was slipping. And thinking about how I couldn't go back, I couldn't stop my story now that I'd started it, even though I was destroying my life a little more with every new word out of my mouth, was unhooking the emotions from the pits of my heart. I was fighting back tears. "How he was going to kill himself. And Naomi too. They were going to do it together. He said she was going through the same heartbreak he was, over—some guy." My God, I almost said Will. "It was shocking. I mean, horrifying, you know? I didn't get the message until, like, noon the next day, and I've been calling and texting them nonstop since then. But nothing. No answer, no nothing."

The guys were staring at me like I was crazy, like shrinks sizing up their inmates in the loony bin. Any second, one of them was going to call bullshit. I just knew it. And then the most painful thought crept through my head. Why shouldn't they? That's what I was thinking. Why shouldn't they call bullshit? They'd be right, after all.

That's when the tears really started to roll. Because I was wrong. In every way a person could be, I was wrong. I was bad. I was evil. I deserved to get caught. I was howling, completely hysterical.

"My God, my God, my God," I kept saying. "I couldn't . . . I didn't . . . So bad . . . So wrong . . ." The words, when they came at all, were strangled in water.

My body slid away from me. I fell off the stool onto the floor, collapsed on the black rubber mat back there, and curled up into a fetal position, wishing it had been me and not my friends who had died.

Through the ocean in my head, I could make out a few muffled signs of life around me. Luke and his friends were asking if I was okay. They were spooked and concerned, embarrassed to be witnesses to such uncoolness. "It's not your fault," one of them mumbled.

Then Luke said, "We should go."

And after a long pause, Ricky said, "We're going to leave our money on the counter. So that you can put it in the drawer when you recover. We're not stealing, okay. We just . . . I mean . . . because—"

"Ricky, just come on," said Toby. "We gotta get out of here."

"Anyway, bye," said Ricky. "Sorry for your loss!"

WILL

Yeah, sure, I'm not stupid. I knew there was a chance people would suspect me. Why wouldn't they? Weird Willy Wanker, you know?

But I tried to play it as cool as I could.

Like, on Monday, I was messing around on the putting green and Lewis came buddying up to me. Just seeing him strut down the hill from the clubhouse got me going. I was thinking, if he even tries to fuck with me, I'll take this club and smash him over the head with it. Completely irrational, but you know? That's where I was right about then. Surging. Anything at all might push me over the edge.

He had that punk-ass smirk plastered across his face, and he was doing his too-cool-for-school walk. I was sure he was going to play that game of his where he pretends to befriend you while subtly pointing out all the ways he thinks he's superior to you. But when he got to me and pulled his wraparound sunglasses up onto his forehead, he had a look in his eye I hadn't seen from him before. Let's call it sympathy.

"Hey man," he said, "tough times. You doing okay?"

"Why wouldn't I be?" I said.

"Craig and Naomi?"

I hadn't heard the rumors flying around town yet. "What about them?" I said.

"Where you been, man? You must be the last person on earth to know. Double suicide."

"Where'd you hear that?"

"Dude. Everywhere! First I heard it was just Naomi—that was this morning. Then, just like, half an hour ago, I got a text from Ricardo that he'd heard Craig was missing too. I guess there was a note, signed in blood by both of them."

Rumors. Gossip. It was absurd, but still, all kinds of crazy stuff flooded into my head then. The images of their bodies stuffed into those wetsuits, and what they might look like now. My sister. Her tears. The look of rage and betrayal that might cloud over her face. The other kids in town—and adults, everybody—whispering into tin cans all connected by strings about *that Will, we always knew he was no good.* Myself in shackles. Myself holding a turret gun, mowing down everyone from here to San Fran.

"Craig," I said, spitting as I spoke. "If there's anyone who deserves to get his head smashed in, it's him." I could have said anything. I wasn't thinking at all, just battling back the rage gushing inside me.

Lewis backed up a step or two, his hands up in front of himself like he was warding me off. "Whoa, dude. That's like total bad mojo," he said. "I don't know about Craig, they haven't found him yet, I think, but, you know, Naomi's head *was* smashed in." The way he was looking at me, it was like he could see something under my skin, a knotted, matted rodent curled up in my chest, and he couldn't tell if it was rabid or not.

"Oh! Jesus!" I said. "That's horrible. You're right. I just . . ." Trailing off, I shook my head gravely, acting like the sad news was just now sinking in. I mumbled something about Asheley, how she and Craig had been having a hard time. Then, for cover, so my face wouldn't betray me in some way, I turned toward my ball and concentrated on putting.

"Have you gone out yet?" said Lewis. "Wanna shoot a round."

I didn't see how I could say no.

One thing about Lewis that worked in my favor is that he's such a bro that there was no way he was going to interrogate me. His imagination only goes three ways: talking shit about girls, recapping the highlights off of SportsCenter, and mocking you for whatever weakness he thinks he's found. As we wandered from hole to hole, I kept waiting for him to surprise me with a question about Craig or Naomi, or with some bit of information he'd forgotten to tell me, something that would trap me into incriminating myself, but he didn't let me down. I was playing like shit, and through the whole front nine, the only conversations we had consisted of him making catcalls and riding me about my game.

Unless he was hiding his suspicions from me, thinking through what I'd said to him on the putting green and watching me for further evidence. Silently putting the pieces together.

By the time we'd reached the fourteenth hole—the little par three where I'd hit my hole in one during the Invitational—I was feeling like I couldn't take much more. The pressure inside me was full to bursting. For the past three holes, I'd been sure I was about to throw up.

The fact that he was kicking my ass just made it worse.

Teeing off with my five iron, I knocked the ball long, into the waist-high grass behind the green.

"Let me show you how it's done, son," Lewis said. Then he finessed his ball beautifully, setting himself up for a birdie, eight feet from the hole.

Prick.

I spent the next fifteen minutes whacking at the grass in search of my ball, but I came up with nothing. It had completely disappeared. And the longer I looked and the more obvious it was that I'd never find the ball, the more bitter I became about Lewis and how he'd taken me off my game with his comments about Craig and Naomi. And this led me back to the thoughts I'd been having earlier, the images of dead bodies and destroyed lives and my total impotence, my utter inability to control Asheley's feelings.

Next thing I knew, I was smashing my club against the trunk of the oak tree out there, just bludgeoning it, doing to it what I wanted to do to Lewis. But the tree was a whole lot stronger than me. All I ended up doing was twisting my club up like a pipe cleaner.

I'll say this: it felt good. By the time I was done, I was calm as can be.

"Dude, you should lay off those steroids," said Lewis.

I saw my opening and I took it. "God, sorry, man. I guess I'm all wound up. I think I'm in shock. Thinking about Naomi and Craig. What they did. It's got me all fucked up. You know? Naomi, fine, I feel bad for her and whatever, but I didn't really know her that well, but Craig, I mean, you know? He dated my sister. She—" Here the truth caught in my throat, but I pushed it out. "She *loved* him. And hearing he went and killed himself, it's just gonna destroy her. Know what I mean?"

Lewis didn't say a thing. He just stared at me, sizing up that rodent in my gut again.

"Man," he said. "You've got problems."

Like I didn't know that.

We didn't say another word to each other throughout the rest of our round. What more was there to say? He suspected me, and he knew I knew he suspected me. The only question was who would he tell and what could I do about it?

Unless that was just me overreacting.

Paranoia. Man, it's a killer.

ASHELEY

I was breaking up inside. I knew that, eventually, I'd spill everything—I didn't know who I'd tell, and I didn't know when, but at some point, it was all going to come tumbling out. The guilt was just too much. And I couldn't grieve as long as I was keeping it all a secret.

And on top of that, there was the other guilt I'd feel if I *did* tell. What would happen to Will? What would they do to him? What would he do to himself? To me?

No matter what I did, I'd end up being a bad person, somehow.

WILL

By the end of the week, the rumors were flying all over the place, on chat sites like The Bay where everyone hung out, on Facebook, on everybody's Twitter feeds. And even though I don't do any of that crap, I could feel the pressure. There were all sorts of variations on what happened, but the basic idea was that Craig and Naomi had been depressed for weeks and then offed themselves. Fine. If that's how they wanted to play it, that was fine with me.

It was destroying Asheley, though.

There was hardly any real news—like legit news, something more than kids talking—about what the cops had discovered and how they were investigating. At least in the press, the two things were being presented as unrelated. There was the story the day Naomi's body had been found. And another one three days later about how Craig was missing—turns out his dad came up out of whatever hole he'd been hiding in and checked in on the shack they lived in.

Maybe you don't know this: Craig's mom had died way back when he was six and he'd been raised, if you could call it that, by his dad, a pothead surfer flake who spent most of his time floating from one girlfriend's apartment to another. He'd stop in for a change of clothes, or to drop off some cash maybe, once every month and a half or so, but Craig was basically alone most of the time. When Surfer Dude saw the article about Naomi, he remembered, *whoa, wait, I've got a kid somewhere*, and he went off to try to find him. He'd made the evening news, looking tragic, and vamped it up about how his precious baby boy had disappeared.

Anyway, that was it. There was a whole lot of frothing and crying, but no news that helped me in any way. It made me wonder, what were they hiding, and how close were they to figuring out the truth? Maybe this was all some huge elaborate trap. Maybe the whole town was waiting for me to slip up. And this was a frustrating place for me to be. It was paralyzing. My brain was spinning constantly around the need to prove my innocence, but I couldn't do anything, I couldn't take action, because if I did, that would be a sure way to get them to suspect me. Know what I mean? It would be like climbing up onto the roof of the school and waving my arms around, shouting into a megaphone, "Not it, not it! I didn't do it," which obviously would mean that I did.

So think about that for a quick second. Imagine how frantic that made me inside. I might have still looked pretty normal to everybody else, but I wasn't feeling normal at all anymore.

The only thing that kept me together was that I knew I had to be strong for Asheley.

ASHELEY

When I got home from work on Saturday, Will was making me another dinner.

This time he'd cleared off the dining room table—the first time that had happened since I can't remember when. He'd gotten rid of the stacks of cups from the party and scrubbed away the sticky rings of alcohol and mixer, moved the piles of CDs and game cartridges and instruction manuals, the piles of weekly shoppers and all that, over to the side table under the stairs. He'd pulled out the good china, the heavy expensive silverware. He'd even laid out the heavy burgundy placemats with the gold tasseled fringe—we never used those things; they were for special occasions and in our house special occasions usually got forgotten once Mom had a couple, ten drinks in her. And the candles! He'd pulled out the wrought iron candelabra with the curling leaf patterns running up its spines.

I swear, it was like he was trying to bribe me. To keep me happy. Like he was afraid I might turn on him now. I have to say, though, it was sort of charming. He was working so hard for his pats on the head. Except I was too jumbled to appreciate it.

Before the meal, there was San Andreas cheese and olives and a baguette. San Andreas is my favorite; it's so buttery and smooth. Even then, though, I wasn't hungry. I hadn't been able to eat much of anything for days.

I tried to play along, to show my appreciation. A nibble here. A nibble there.

Salad from Keith's organic garden in the backyard.

Fancy chardonnay from the Napa Valley. He brought that out right before the main course and he made a big show of pouring it into the glasses like he was a pro, the napkin over the arm, the little twist of the bottle so it wouldn't drip, everything. Then he held his glass up and proposed a toast.

Did I say he was manic? He was completely manic. Jerky and bouncy, even more than usual.

"To us!" he said. He was speaking really fast. "Wonder Twin powers, unite!"

I chinked glasses with him. I tried to smile. But the joke was getting old. Honestly? I wasn't feeling much like his Wonder Twin anymore. More like the poor cousin trapped in the attic— Harry Potter, without the magic of Hogwarts to look forward to.

He went on. "I think, from what I've been seeing on the news and whatever that we're gonna be okay. It's been almost a week since they found Naomi and they're still talking suicide.

And Craig? I mean, Craig must be shark food by now. They've got nothing. Nada. Right? I mean, right?"

I nodded. "Right," I said, flatly. I couldn't meet his eye.

"But look at me!" he said. "That means we're going to be okay. We're going to be okay! You and me and the wide blue yonder! We got away with it. They'd be coming after us by now if that was what they were going to do. So . . . we did it!" He was hopping back and forth, grinning, this crazy, giddy expression on his face.

And then he grabbed my hands and started dancing. Actually dancing! And singing that stupid "I Got You Babe" song.

My friends were dead. My *boyfriend*. Dead. They were dead. And he wanted to dance and do karaoke. It was all I could do not to throw my wine in his face.

I'm sorry. I'm doing it again. I shouldn't be crying like this.

So, yeah. For the main course, he made this risotto he'd seen on the Food Network. Parmesan, asparagus, Italian sausage. My God. I don't know how Mario Batalli does it, but I'm sure it's not the same as what Will put together. Talk about salty. A deer would have cringed tasting that stuff. And half of it was burned, too. It was totally nasty. It took all I had just to swallow two bites.

"You like it?" he asked me.

"Sure." What else could I say?

He was shoveling it down like it was the best thing he'd ever eaten. And he kept babbling, throwing back the wine, going on and on about what we were going to do now, since we were free and together and we had all summer now to do whatever we wanted.

He had this idea of the two of us taking off somewhere, going to some resort where he could play golf all day and I could lie on the beach, tanning and reading and listening to my iPod. He kept throwing the names of islands out there: Jamaica. St. Barts. Maui. Whatever.

And I nodded along. I tried to placate him. "Yeah, we could do that. Yeah, that would be nice." Just trying to shut him up and cool him down somehow.

But whatever I did, it wasn't enough for him. He could tell I wasn't into this game he was playing. "Are you okay, Ash?" he asked. "Aren't you a little bit excited?"

"Of course," I said, but I wasn't. I was totally freaked out by him. The Will I trusted, the one who was moody and sad sometimes because he cared so deeply for people's fragile emotions, the one who tied himself in knots trying to do what was right, that Will was gone, and the one who'd replaced him was, like, a crazed monster. Fixated on me in all these ways that had nothing to do with the real me at all.

Seriously, I was almost wishing Mom was back from rehab so she could mock him and remind him what a small, feeble boy he was.

Or maybe not that. But I was definitely wishing Dad was around. That he knew what had happened to us since Mom had driven him away. I just knew, I was positive, that if he knew, if there were some sort of camera, or a magic bird that flew above the house and watched us, reporting back to him about every little thing that happened to us, he would have raced up to help. He would have put up his shield and held us safe behind it. That's what I wanted. I was aching for him. Wishing beyond wish that the front door would fling open and he'd come charging in to make everything better.

Yeah right. Whatever.

After he cleared the plates and everything off the table, Will came up behind me and put his hands on my shoulders. He leaned in and kissed me on the cheek, and I don't know, this terrible feeling raced through my body. I shuddered and my head knocked him accidentally on the nose. I think he was trying to whisper something in my ear, but what, I don't know. It got lost in the sound of my body shivering.

Then he started massaging the knots in my neck. Giving me a back rub.

I don't think I've ever felt so lonely.

He was kneading his thumbs in these long slow arcs across my shoulders, and drawing circles on my collarbones with his fingers.

I tried to shake him off, but he didn't notice.

Finally, I shoved him.

"I don't want this," I said. "Can't you see that?"

The look on his face. It was like I'd slapped him. Or like I'd taken his heart and thrown it off a cliff. He just crumbled. Reeling back, slumping dejected on the arm of the couch. I thought he was going to cry.

"I'm sorry," I said. "I just, I'm overwhelmed."

Then I reached out and squeezed his hand so he'd understand.

"Wonder Twins," I said, throwing him as much of a smile as I could manage.

WILL

That was nice, rubbing her shoulders. The rumors and the lying and the putting a shiny face on had been getting to Ash all week, and her muscles were knotted in thirty different ways. I could feel them loosening and relaxing under my fingers and this was a relief. Finally, I was doing something right, helping her feel better instead of worse.

And I could tell, she was really appreciating it.

Who knows where that might have led as the night progressed. I'd rented *The Hangover*, which I knew she'd been wanting to see. And I'd pulled another bottle of wine up from the basement. Maybe we would have curled up together on the couch and laughed a little. Had a little bit of something like normal. For once. Finally. I was looking forward to a little bit of snuggling.

But no, cause who showed up, right then? Keith. Of course. It was like his house arrest bracelet had started blinking, telling him, *danger, danger, they're turning toward happy now*, and he had to rush over to ruin our night.

He did his usual nosing around the kitchen, spooned himself up a bowl of risotto, shoved the six pack of near-beer he'd brought with him into the fridge—all except one, which he popped open on the handle of the silverware drawer. Then, carrying the dregs of the salad in one hand and balancing the rest of his loot in the other, he wandered over to sit at the table with us.

"My garden," he said, picking soggy leaves and cucumbers out of the bowl with his fingers. "Real food for real people."

"You can really taste the difference," said Asheley. She didn't seem disappointed to see him. Not as disappointed as she should have been, anyway.

As he chomped at the salad, Keith was swaying back and forth, like, going into a food trance, muttering about organic this and organic that, and Asheley was nodding along, yessing him, sort of, encouraging him. I'm sure she was just being polite, but still, it was ugly to watch. Keith with his mouth full, flecks of radish and tomato dribbling back into the bowl under his chin, and Ash just rolling with it, like she didn't have the spirit to stand up for herself anymore. Like things had gotten so hard that I had to do everything.

When he turned to the risotto, he took one bite and made a face. "Great job with the spicing," he said. He downed half his near-beer and took the bowl of risotto back to the kitchen and dumped it in the compost pail. "So," he said, "what do we got cooking tonight?"

"You just threw it away," I said.

"Oh, sorry, I guess I'm speaking the wrong lingo," he said. "What's the hookup? What's on the agenda?"

Before I could tell him that the agenda consisted of marching him back out to his car so we could enjoy ourselves in peace, Ash said, "*The Hangover*. Seen it?"

And then we were stuck with him. Ash had given him an in. I still don't understand why she was willing to let him play daddy for us that night. It's not like her. She disliked him as much as I did.

Anyway, I put the movie on and as the opening credits rolled, he started in about, "Speaking of hangovers, your mom's finally starting to get over hers. I was out there today and we took a nice walk around the grounds. We even saw a lizard." He flicked his tongue in and out a few times and let his eyes roll around in their sockets. "She's writing in a journal, really working out the crap in her life. She's got that sparkle she used to have again."

So that's what he was up to. He was delivering the news. Mom would be home soon. I wondered what *that sparkle* might look like. If it would be the same sparkle she'd had when I was young. I hoped so, for her sake. That didn't mean I was looking forward to her coming home, though. I liked having the house to myself and Asheley.

"Are you going to talk through the whole movie?" I asked.

He adjusted his glasses and pulled his chin down into his neck in a kind of *excuuuse me* gesture.

The thing that really got me was that Asheley gave me a critical look too. "You can always rewind," she said.

And Keith winked at her. Really! He winked and he slouched back and threw his arm wide along the back of the couch, like he was inviting her to snuggle in while we watched the show.

Jesus.

I didn't even care about the movie by then. The evening was ruined already, so what was the point? The thing I cared about was keeping an eye on Keith.

I could feel myself pulling inward. If I'd thought I could do it without them noticing, if I'd been able to do it without leaving Asheley alone with Keith, I would have wandered off to the cliff. Hung out there alone, throwing pebbles out into the bay. Thinking things through. It's not like I could do that though, so I just sat there, apart from them, pretending to watch the movie, remembering all the ways Keith had annoyed me throughout my life, all the times he'd lingered out in the yard, digging up weeds and watching as Ash and I played, all the evenings back before he quit drinking when he'd been slugging beers in front of the tube, watching those women's college basketball games he liked so much. Where was Mom in all of this? Almost every memory I could think of was missing Mom. There was Keith washing his truck and spraying Asheley with the hose. There was Keith picking us up from school. There he was tooling around in the shed, while Ash sunbathed in the backyard. It was always Asheley. That's where his attention went. Every second of every day he was at the house. Asheley, Asheley, Asheley.

And why? I knew why. I mean, obviously. Ash is a sexy girl. She's spunky. She's like sunlight. And he wanted some of that. He wanted to take it and blot it out.

Halfway through the movie, I was snapped back out of my thoughts by this:

"Hey, you know what would make this comedy funnier? A little bit of the *cucaracha*. What do you say, Asheley? Want to get stoned with your mom's old man?"

"No!" I said. I almost shouted it.

"Relax, Will. You can come too if you want," he said.

I would have, too, but I figured, if I did, he'd be on to me.

That, and I was filling up with so much rage that I was afraid of what I might do to him.

ASHELEY

Will stayed inside, brooding on the couch. He was acting like a baby, petulant, stewing in his self-pity. I mean, I understand, Keith could be annoying and whatever, but you know? He was there now. Big whoop. It's not like he was that bad. I was actually sort of happy to see him. In his loopy way, he was a great distraction.

Outside, the two of us sat in the deck chairs on the porch and gazed out at the shadows of the backyard. There was a nice breeze, not too cool, but still refreshing. And the moon was really big—like a half moon, but the line between the light and dark on it was crisp and if you stared hard enough you could almost see the craters on it.

He lit up a joint and took a few puffs, then held it out to me, but I said, no, I'm cool. Watching him get stoned was one thing. I'd done that a thousand times. But actually smoking up with him? That was too weird. I'm not much of a pothead anyway. I've only done it, like, twice, with Craig, and both times, it didn't seem to do much of anything. I think I'm immune to it.

Keith took his glasses off and washed them on his shirt, and then, instead of putting them back on, he held them there in his lap. He kept looking at me, like looking deep, staring, not in a creepy way, more like he was trying to dig inside of me and pull out some nugget hidden in there, hold it up, examine it, figure it out. His eyes, without the glasses on, were terribly sad.

"How you holding up?" he said.

"I'm fine," I said. I was feeling good about having him around, but not *that* good. Not good enough to go spilling my soul to him.

He just kept staring at me. "Really?" he said.

I nodded.

"'Cause you seem not so good."

"I am," I said.

But then, I don't know. The expression on his face. It was so . . . kind. I sort of lost it. My face went all blubbery and I started quietly sobbing.

Keith took a long drag on his joint. He put his glasses back on. He reached out toward me with an open hand. "I thought so," he said. He waited for me to take his hand. "You sure you're okay?"

A new rush of sadness tumbled through me. "No," I said. More like a squeak than a word.

"Hey," he said, "hey." He squeezed out the cherry on his joint and slipped the roach into his pocket, then standing up, he said again, "Hey."

And I let him hug me. I needed *someone* to hug me. Someone other than Will. He patted my back a little and just held me, whispering, "Okay, now. It's okay," over and over. I must have sobbed on his shoulder for like ten minutes. It was completely sopping wet by the time I got it together and pulled my head away.

"Wanna talk about it?" he said.

I nodded. Everything was flooding up in me and I couldn't control any of it.

Then I thought of Will. I'd almost forgotten him in there. I felt a shot of panic—fear—thinking maybe he was listening in somehow. Watching us at least. Making assumptions. When I glanced through the sliding glass door, though, he was still brooding, staring at the TV, totally wrapped up in his dark mood.

Keith saw me look, and he glanced in too. "Wanna take a walk?" he said.

I nodded again. But where would we walk to? The pathway through the woods? The cliffs? I couldn't bear the idea of going there. "Maybe just a little ways out into the backyard, though," I said. "Just far enough—"

"I understand," he said, throwing a half-nod toward Will. "Grab your chair."

We dragged our lawn chairs down the slope to the fire pit at the far corner of the yard and situated them so we were facing the deck—that way if Will slipped out to find us, we'd see him coming. We sat back in our chairs, staring up at the sky. Thin wispy clouds were floating up there, frayed white lines cutting across the stars.

And I told him everything. Well, sort of. Not exactly. I told him about Craig and Naomi. How Naomi's body had washed up and all that. This wasn't news to him. He watches the news. He reads the paper. And how Craig was missing. How I hadn't heard from him. I didn't lie exactly. I mean, I didn't say anything that wasn't strictly true. But I made sure to stick to the facts that had been reported. I didn't mention the roles Will and I had played.

Anyway, that's not what mattered—the facts, I mean. What mattered was that Craig and Naomi were gone and I was a total wreck about it.

I told Keith how I felt like my world had gone crazy. How things had started to seem like they didn't mean anything. How everything tasted empty and gray. And how I felt, not numb, exactly, more like the opposite, like my emotions were so strong and overwhelming that they became a constant ache, they became all one unending painful thing, and I wondered, would this ever change? Or would I be submerged in this pain for the rest of my life?

"Kiddo," he said, "I can't answer that for you. It might stick around. Or it might not. It might soften a little and mix itself up with everything else you've got inside you, become another of those things that hurt to think about."

He went quiet for a minute. His face, in the shadows of the yard, looked so old, like, filled up with the history of his own pain. He reminded me of a redwood, like he'd seen the sad things time sent rambling past him, and their history was etched in his skin like furrows in bark.

"I wish it weren't so, though," he said quietly. "Your mom

and me. We want you kids to be . . . okay. It might sometimes not seem that way, but . . . there it is."

He was crying. I'd never seen him cry before. He didn't make a sound. He just shook a little in the shoulders and fumbled with the buttons on his shirt. Then he started to sing in a hoarse whispery voice.

Blue, blue windows behind the stars,
Yellow moon on the rise.
Big birds flying across the sky,
Throwing shadows on our eyes.
Leave us,
Helpless, helpless, helpless, helpless.

"Neil Young," he said. "He knows how you feel." And he went quiet again.

It was weird. For the first time in my life, I felt totally comfortable around him, more than comfortable. *Comforted.* Like all that time I'd thought he was just hanging out 'cause he didn't have anything better to do, all those awkward and sort of icky ways he'd look at me—I'd misunderstood everything about him. He'd been trying to, I don't know, *care* about me or something.

Then I started crying too. 'Cause, really, who'd ever cared about me before? It didn't even matter if he didn't know what to do. What mattered was that he tried.

I reached across to him and held his big calloused hand.

He smiled—just for a second. He squeezed my fingers. "I'm sorry," he said.

We sat there for I don't know how long.

Then finally, Will's shadow appeared behind the sliding glass door. He stood there for a moment, watching us. Sliding it open a crack, he stuck his head out. "Are you ever going to come back in? Jeez!"

Keith raised an eyebrow at me. "Man, I'm totally stoned," he said. "No way I'm making my way out of here tonight."

"That's okay," I said. "There's always Mom's room."

"Exactomento," he said. "Maybe I'll do those dishes for you guys before I crash. Earn my keep."

He stood up and stretched, clasping his hands above his head and arching his back like a little kid.

I just hung there, watching him go.

Halfway to the house he turned back toward me. "You coming?"

"No," I said. "I think I'm going to sit here for a while more."

And that's what I did. I curled my legs up into my chair and stayed out there for like an hour or more. Not really doing anything. Just sitting. Just feeling. Wondering what Keith would do if I told him the rest of what had happened with Craig and Naomi. Thinking, maybe I should.

WILL

Maybe an hour later, Asheley finally came back inside.

Keith had already skulked off to Mom's room to pass out. Not much I could do about it. It was a classic ask-Mom-if-Dad-won't-give-you-what-you-want sort of thing, and Ash had already told him he could stay. I'd been hanging around the living room, waiting, trying to keep my imagination in check, wondering what the hell he'd said to her to get her to go soft, and what that might mean for our future plans together. By the time she came in, I'd worked myself up into . . . I was a mess.

"What was that all about?" I asked her.

"It's nice out there. I was just hanging out. Thinking. Watching the stars. This squirrel was playing around on the roof of the shed. It was interesting."

"Not that. You know what I'm talking about."

She was playing dumb, scrunching up her face in a kind of confused expression.

"With Keith." Even though the light in Mom's room was off, I knew he might be listening in, so I whispered this. Sort of hissed it, actually. Like I said, I was pissed.

"That was nothing. We were just talking."

"Yeah, obviously. But why? I mean, why would you want to . . . he's, I mean, did he try to touch you?"

"No," she said. She sat down on the step leading up to the door and I could tell she was uncomfortable. Her posture was too perfect. Guarded. Tense.

"That's a surprise," I said. "Anyway, even if he didn't, he wanted to. I know it." A flash image of Keith walking his fingers up Asheley's thigh burned through my mind and I spasmed into a whole new kind of anger. "He's been looking for the chance forever. What? Did he sweet-talk you? Tell you how much he cares about how hard it is to be you in the world? I wouldn't trust him. No way would I trust him."

She shot a glance at Mom's door and she shushed me. "He's fine," she said.

I shouted, "No!" Then more quietly, I said, "He's not fine. He's got a thing for you. It makes me sick to my stomach. The thought that he might try to—"

"Will! Will, listen to me!" she said. "You're talking crazy. Keith's just trying to, I don't know, be a dad or something. He's awkward, okay, but he's not bad. He comes around every few days or so, and he scratches his head and asks how we're doing, and I mean, so what? You know? Tell him we're doing fine. Smile for him. Let him walk away thinking he's accomplished something. How hard is that? And then you and me, we can keep on doing things just like we have been. You know? Trust me. We're a team. You and me. He's just a guy who shows up every once in a while."

Something released in me when she reminded me that we were a team. Some of that anger leaked out and I felt slightly better. At least I hadn't lost her. That was a relief. But, still, what had she said to him? I don't know why I hadn't thought about this earlier, but the real issue was whether or not she had let slip anything that might lead him to realize what we'd been up to. I mean, I knew she was having a hard time with all that, and if she trusted Keith now, who knows . . .

"Did he ask about Craig?" I said.

Totally not the right thing to do. She almost looked like she was going to come flailing at me with her fists.

"Drop it, okay, Will?" she said. "We talked. I can talk to whoever I want. You don't own me. But no, okay? We didn't talk about Craig. Or Naomi. And even if we did, you think I'd be so stupid as to tell him what really happened? Come on!"

She was keeping something from me. It was there in her face, in the way she was trying so hard to get me to believe her. But what? I had no idea. All I knew was that she'd shifted away from me, psychologically, emotionally. She was inching away, getting ready to abandon me.

Then her face went soft—the love returned to it. I almost teared up I was so relieved.

"Give me your hands," she said.

I did, and she held them, lightly and looked deep into my eyes.

"You really think I'd let Keith touch me? You really think I'd ever betray you? Trust me a little bit," she said, "Okay? I'm a big girl. We're in this together. Whatever happens, I'll be right there with you. Okay? You believe me, right? Will, you're my best friend."

"I'll try," I said. It was the best I could do.

"I love you, Will," she said. The tenderness in her smile when she said this was maybe the nicest thing I'd ever seen in my life.

"Okay, I'm going to bed. You should go to bed, too," she said then.

As she passed me on her way toward the stairs, she paused. She took my face between her hands and tilted it upward and she kissed me on the cheek. And then, like a message written in the sand, her smile faded.

"Really," she said, "come to bed."

"I will," I said. "Soon."

I wanted to believe her. You have no idea how badly I wanted to believe her. And the more I thought about it, after she was gone and I was alone again in the living room, the more I understood that it wasn't her I had to worry about. She was as devoted to me as I was to her. The problem was with Keith. He'd already started trying to insinuate himself into her trust. Now that he had an in, I was sure he'd exploit it. And then what? Would Asheley really be able to fend him off?

ASHELEY

The next morning I had to get up at eight to open Milky Moo's. Even though I'd gone into overdrive the night before, begging Will to just be normal for once, to, like, not do any of the crazy shit that might be rattling around in his brain, I was worried anyway. I couldn't control him and I couldn't warn Keith about what he might do to him without spilling everything that had already happened. So it ended up with me laying awake all night, itchy and panicked, afraid of what Will might have planned for us next. I think I got maybe two hours' sleep, tops.

I don't know how I managed to get myself out of bed—I was so exhausted. But I did. I took my shower. I pulled on my corny black-and-white-splotched Milky Moo's uniform. I got myself ready.

The house was quiet as I headed downstairs. Will was asleep. Keith was asleep—I peeked into Mom's room to check on him, because—well, you can imagine why I did that. The morning sunlight was pouring in through the skylight, bright golden cones of almost solid brilliance. It was really pretty, actually. It made me wonder if maybe things would change that day. Maybe a little air and light would come seeping in and open a little goodness up into my world.

Fat chance. The first thing that happened once I got downstairs was I looked up the *Central Valley News* on my computer to see if there was any new news on Craig and Naomi, and turns out they'd finally found Craig's body. It was weird, seeing the headline. "Second Local Teen Found Dead in Morro Bay." I didn't feel much of anything. And then I felt this kind of creeping horror at myself for not feeling anything. If you only knew how tired I was.

Driving to work, I kept thinking I saw things that weren't there—like, something would move in the corner of my eye, and then when I looked at it, it turned out to just be a mailbox or a shrub or something. It was like there were hidden spirits in the world, and in my exhaustion, my mind wasn't blocking them out like it usually did.

At work it was slow. Once I'd gotten the soft-serve machines running and done all the prep stuff—setting up the topping containers and putting the money in the register and all that— there wasn't much for me to do but just sit there, listening to my iPod, leafing through the book I'd brought along with me, nodding off and jolting my head back up every ten minutes or so. Once in a while, someone would come in, like an ex-hippie—we have loads of them—in jeans and a peasant blouse out for a stroll with her barefoot, dirty-faced four-year-old granddaughter, and they'd quiz me on where we got our milk from and whether or not we made the ice cream in-house and all sorts of things, whether or not our chocolate sprinkles were organic. Then, after about fifty free samples, they'd order a small cone that the kid would either plop onto the floor or just stare at, complaining, "I'm not hungry, now."

Yeah, good times, I know. Welcome to my world.

And I kept seeing things. Like, ants and cockroaches crawling across the counters that turned out to not be there when I looked closely.

Or—and this was the scary one—splotches of blood in the ice cream. Really. That happened, like, four or five times. I'd look up from whatever I was doing and there'd be these oozy red clumps of frozen blood lodged in the gallon containers, and I'd think, my God, the things Will and I did have started to leak out into the physical world, like all these things around me, natural or man-made, are pushing back at me for what I've done. Then I'd look again and it would turn out that what I'd been seeing was just cherries and strawberry swirl.

I was really falling apart. I mean, I was shaking. I was afraid to look at anything. I couldn't carry a thought for more than half a second.

Then, to top it all off, sometime around ten thirty, Mom called me.

Given how my day had been going, this was almost a relief. Instead of sending her to voicemail and finding out what she wanted before talking to her, I actually answered.

"Ash!" she said. Her voice was wispy and thin, just hearing it filled me with a kind of almost-happiness.

She told me how things had been going at Hope Hill, all about the activities and therapy sessions and all that. She talked about how hard it had been to face the carnage she'd created in my life and Will's life. It's not like she said she was sorry, but I could hear, in her plain, undramatic descriptions of her thinking about her experiences now that she wanted my forgiveness.

"It sounds like you've been working really hard," I said.

"Oh, can it," she said. "You don't have to pump me up. Anyway, that's not why I'm calling. I've had about all I can take of me, me, me. It's time for me to start thinking about you."

Hesitantly, I said, "Oh, I'm fine."

"That's not what I hear from Keith. I hear you two had a purging, deep talk last night."

"We did."

"He's a good man," Mom said. "A space case, yes, but tender. He's maybe the kindest person I've ever met. I'm glad you two were able to connect a little. Nobody knows how to listen like Keith. There's not a judgmental bone in his body."

I wasn't going to cry. No matter how overtired I was, no matter how overwhelming everything was, no way would I stand there and cry *again*—especially not to my sad, broken mother.

"And then, this news today about Craig. I figured I had to call. I can't imagine how you're holding it together," she said. "If it were me, I'd be so shit-faced by now that I'd probably not even know my own name."

"Well, that's the difference between you and me, Mom."

I meant this jokingly, and believe it or not, she got it. She laughed.

"Amen to that." She went silent for a minute, then she said, "Really, Ash, I need you to know that I'd kill to be there rocking you to sleep right now." Before I could protest, she went on. "I know, I know. That's not worth much right now. But it's true. I wasn't completely gone this past year. I know how important Craig was to you. I mean, yeah, okay, there were tears a lot of the time. There was sometimes shouting going on behind your closed door. I caught all that. But it was the exception, wasn't it, hon?"

So, so quietly, I said, "Yeah." That's right about when I lost all my defenses and just started bawling. And I couldn't believe it! She hung on the phone and listened. It was like she was holding me. I never thought I'd see that happen!

When I'd cried myself out, she cooed at me a little and then she said, "We'll get through this. It's going to take a while, but we'll get through this."

"It's so *hard* though," I said.

"But you're tough. You've had to deal with me. That's enough to make anybody strong."

It was like she was holding an image of a better me up in front of me, and I wanted to believe I could be that person. That got me going again with the tears. I missed her. I loved her. Wow. I'd never thought I'd be willing to say that.

"When are you coming home?" I asked her.

"They're telling me three more weeks. We'll see. I'm doing good, but it can only go as fast as it goes. I'm trying, but—"

"I love you, Mom," I said. I couldn't stop myself. I had to tell her before the feeling faded.

There was a pause, then when she spoke again, she did so carefully, deliberately. "Don't say that, Ash. Don't try to soften it for me. I know what I've done to your life. If you're going to forgive me, at least let me earn it."

"I just want you to—"

"Oop, they're calling me," she said. "I have to go. Bye. I'll call again soon."

And she was gone. I knew her well enough to realize nobody had been calling her. That was just her excuse. She shied away from mushy stuff, especially when it was directed at her. That's fine. She'd heard me at least. That's what counted. One bright spot in a pretty shitty day.

Then the ants and cockroaches and the splotches of blood were back. I had visions of this going on for the rest of my life, getting worse, of me losing touch with reality completely, turning into a crazy, raving lunatic seeing signs of her own guilt written all over the world.

Something had to change. *I* had to change. The first step—the only right thing for me to do—was to confess to somebody about what we'd done. To Keith, maybe. Mom was right, he was a kind man. He cared about me and he cared about Will and I was sure he'd see how complicated this all was. I wasn't sure if he'd know what to do, but he'd try, and then, hopefully, we could figure out what to do next together.

WILL

Keith had been heavy. I'd only managed to topple him over the edge, lodging him half in and half out of the water. Once it was over, I stood on my cliff for a very long time, staring down into the bay, watching the water crash against the rocks, watching it reach its hand out and pull Keith's body slowly down into its dark current. I thought about how heavy that water was, how powerful it was.

Then I staggered away, into the woods, following the path back toward the house. I was exhausted, physically, mentally, emotionally. Totally spent, like I'd come to the end of a triathlon and suddenly now, with my adrenaline receding, the bruising truth of what I'd put myself through was finally registering in my consciousness. My legs wobbled under me. My muscles twitched. There were aches in my upper arms like I'd never experienced.

Keith had put up more fight than I'd expected from him—there was a lot of strength inside that dried-out beef jerky frame of his. Even after I'd gotten in a few good hits with my golf club, he'd managed to throw me off of him, and we'd tumbled and flailed over each other quite a bit. I had cuts and scratches. I could tell already that I was going to have some bruised ribs.

When I got to the shed, I paused briefly to wipe the sweat from my forehead and discovered that it wasn't sweat at all but blood. Lots of blood. I dug my fingers through my hair, ran them along my forehead and scalp, trying to figure out how bad the damage was. The cut seemed deep, and long, but beyond that, hard to tell.

And here's the thing. I wanted to feel bad for Keith. Part of me couldn't help being sentimental, remembering those few times throughout my childhood when he'd done what he could to pay attention to me. He'd taught me how to use a hammer and a saw and a screwdriver. We'd built a rickety little side table together once, back when I was eleven years old or so. I had a few memories like this, where he was doing some vaguely fatherly thing with me, introducing me to songs by his favorite bands—Deep Purple, Led Zeppelin—baiting hooks for me and showing me how to cast a fishing line off the edge of his houseboat down at the docks.

And he'd done more for Mom than my father ever had. No question about that. He'd pulled her away from fights out at the bars. He'd driven her, limp and moaning, halfway to passing out, home from wherever it was she might have been, never once roughing her up, never once being anything but careful and tender with her as he draped her arm across his shoulders and walked her through doorways and up stairs.

In a lot of ways he hadn't been such a bad guy.

But not in the way that counted most. When it came to Asheley, he was a total perv. Lecherous. A revolting dirty old man. I can't count how many times I'd watched him sprawl in the rotating chair in the living room, a near-beer in his hand, his eyes hidden behind those oversized dark glasses of his, thinking nobody was noticing how completely focused he was on Asheley's every twist and turn on her pillow on the floor, on how her butt looked in her shorts and how her tank top fell just the slightest bit at her bust when she leaned over in just the right way. When he went to hug her, I'd watch him let his hand slip just a little too far down her back, his fingers lingering there at the base of her spine. It was disgusting. Unforgivable.

Totally unforgivable.

And except when I mentioned it to her in private, Asheley was oblivious. That's the thing about her. She so wants to believe that people have kind intentions—she needs to believe it. I responded to all the shit we've been through by sharpening myself, learning the danger signs and keeping vigilant look out for them. But her response was the total opposite. She bent herself all up trying to find the good in the world. Refusing to see how ugly other people really are. Unless someone comes out and blatantly attacks her, she's going to believe they're basically good.

But they're not. People aren't good. Men especially. And men who are all hopped up with desire? Forget it. They'd do anything, connive and sweet-talk and fill your head with all sorts of happy promises to get what they want. Then, once you've let your guard down, once you're open to them, they'll unsheathe their claws and tear you apart. Taking whatever they want from you. Your body. Your soul. Everything. They're ruthless. They'll savage you.

I'm glad I killed Keith, if that's what it took to keep Asheley safe. I'd do it again. I'd kill anyone who tried to hurt her. Who tried to convince her to give them her body, and for what? So they could get their jollies for a couple hours? So they could take her and use her and throw her away?

And they would. Ash was at that age, and she had that trusting smile. Every man out there was going to try his luck.

But how does somebody protect the ones he loves from an enemy that massive? Is it even possible?

Doesn't matter. Doesn't matter one bit. Who was it—Mitch Hedberg?—who said, "If you love someone, lock them up and throw away the key"? Whoever it was, they were right. And the time had come—the danger was way, way too high—for me to take that kind of preventative action to ensure that no one would ever hurt Asheley.

The trick was to get her to go along with it. To get her to realize this was the best of all choices. While I washed the blood off my face and hands, while I wrapped my drenched, torn clothes in a plastic bag, I stewed on this question. What to do? How to do it?

The cut on my forehead was pretty bad. I doused it with water, then hydrogen peroxide, then I sprayed Bactine on it. It started up in my hair where it wasn't visible, but the last inch or so extended down over my temple. No way to hide it, not even if I parted my hair to the side. But I didn't bandage it. Better to not draw attention to it. If Asheley asked, I'd say I'd been pounding my head on a door, taking my worry about things out on myself. I'd been known to do it before, and she was wise to lame excuses. She'd heard about a billion of them from Mom over the years.

But what to do? Where to go?

The one thing I knew for sure was that we had to leave. Keith, Craig, Naomi—they'd be able to triangulate the three and when they did, the lines would all intersect at Asheley and me.

I packed up a duffel bag of clothes for myself.

Mom was paranoid about banks. Don't ask. Something about them wanting her social security number. And then, also, she was convinced, if her money was in the bank, that the government, or like, the loan collectors who were always after her to pay back her student loans, might be able to just reach in and confiscate it. And I knew, when I was a kid, anyway, she used to keep her cash hidden in her room. So I took a look. I dug around in her room until I found her money in one of the empty shoe boxes in her closet. A couple thousand bucks. That was going to help.

Feeling a little manic, I headed into Asheley's room to pack a bag for her. I took great care in picking out her clothes, folding them, laying them nicely in her fresh pink-, yellow-, and baby-blue-striped rollie bag. I knew exactly what looked best on her, and I made sure to include as many of those things— dirty or not—as I could.

Then, 'cause I knew how much she'd appreciate me for

it, I dug through the pile of clothes on her floor until I found the bright red Stanford sweatshirt she liked so much. It reeked of that talcum powder and lavender smell from the perfume she liked, but then, also, under this, there was a richer scent, a slightly acidic musky smell—the smell of her. I held the sweatshirt to my face and breathed in her essence. It was like smelling salts. It took me down a notch. Folding the sweatshirt up, I placed it in her bag and zipped it up.

What did she love the way I loved her scent? Where did she look when she needed to renew her hope? I wanted to think she looked to me, but I wasn't so sure of that.

On her bedside table, in a plastic frame made of interlocking hearts, was a fading photo of her as a baby, cradled in Dad's arms. I flashed rage for a second seeing the expression on his face. Was that adoration? Pride? Whatever it was, I was sure he'd forgotten all about it.

Then I noticed something I hadn't seen before in the photo.

His T-shirt. Stanford. His alma mater.

My synapses started crackling with connections. I knew what my plan should be and I knew Asheley would be happy to come along.

ASHELEY

I was hunched over the door, my back to the street, rattling the key in the lock that always jams at Milky Moo's, trying to close up for the day, when I heard wheels peeling around the corner behind me, and then an engine gunning, loud, right at me. I turned and fell backward and there was Keith's Eagle, riding right up onto the sidewalk and screeching to a halt. I swear, it came about two inches from hitting me.

Either Keith was in a rage like I'd never seen before, the kind of rage I was pretty sure he wasn't capable of, or it was Will.

It was Will.

Leaving the engine running, he flew out the door and roughly picked me up from the sidewalk, talking fast and low. "You okay? Come on, get in." He had me by the shoulder, his hand clamped tight, steering me toward the passenger door. And he was jittering like he does when he's in a state. Refusing to look me in the eye.

I tried to squirm out of his grasp, I swear, but he wouldn't allow it.

He shoved me in the car and then he raced around and hopped into the driver's seat.

I don't know why I didn't jump out and run. I was scared. Terrified of what he'd do to me if I tried to run. He was completely out of his head. And also, what good would it have done? He's way faster than me. He would have just chased me down and dragged me back.

The other thing was, yeah, I felt responsible in a way. I could just tell he was going to do something bad, if he hadn't already, and I understood that I was the only one who could reach him, the only one who could talk sense to him, and I . . . You know what I mean? I wanted it to stop. All of it. I didn't want anybody else to get hurt.

So, then, we were off, going way too fast, jolting around corners and running stop signs, all of it. Will had both hands on the wheel, squeezing so tightly his fingers were turning white. He was muttering to himself—I have no idea what—like, cursing under his breath at the people who turned to look as we raced past.

I was almost too terrified to think of what to say. I knew I had to be careful. I mean, obviously, he was losing it, and if I said the wrong thing, who knows what would happen.

"Thanks for picking me up," I said.

He grunted in response.

We were heading out of the downtown area, away from the knickknack shops and restaurants and all that into the wider streets that curved through the hills. Moving sort of toward the high school. *Not* toward the house. That's not what was freaking me out the most though. The thing that was freaking me out most of all was the car. I mean, Will had his own car. And if he was driving Keith's, then . . . and that cut on his head, too . . . Just thinking about the possible reasons for this was almost too much for me to take.

"What happened to the Saab?" I asked.

He muttered again.

"I can't understand what you're saying," I said.

He gulped down a big breath, then said, more clearly, "Something's wrong with it."

"And Keith let you run off with his car?"

I couldn't tell if he was nodding or just bouncing his head up and down, counting off the thoughts galloping through his mind.

"How's he going to get to work?" I asked.

"I guess that job's over," he said.

"That was nice of him," I said, "to let you take his car."

"Wasn't it?" he said. Then he glanced at me and winked.

Yeah, I suspected. But, I don't know. I was so focused on keeping him calm. Also, something in the shy wisp of a smile on his face told me not to push the subject any further than I already had. I felt sick to my stomach and I rolled down the window to let in some fresh air. It didn't help.

By now we were shooting along Paradise Drive, almost at the strip mall way on the edge of town.

"Hey, where are we going, anyway?" I said, trying to sound like I was excited to be on an adventure with him.

He followed Paradise Drive up toward Highway 1, then turned onto 41. I knew this route. This was the way we went when we were headed inland toward Bakersfield.

"Will, really? Where are we going?"

In the back seat were a couple of bags. His rubberized sports duffel and an old striped roller bag of mine from when I was thirteen and into large blocky primary colors. I don't know how I hadn't noticed them before.

"We're going somewhere, Will. Obviously. So tell me what's up."

He just kept on driving.

And I started to panic. I was totally losing it.

"Tell me!" I pounded my palm against the seat, the door, the dash. "Tell me!"

He glanced at me, finally. "You really want to know?"

"Do I look like I want to know?"

"It'll ruin the surprise."

"I'm sick of surprises. I hate surprises. This isn't fun for me, Will. Really."

"Hey—" He patted my knee. "Don't . . . It's . . ." He kept looking over at me, truly concerned. "Okay. So you're not going to believe this, but I got a call from Dad today. Really. Turns out he's been trying to get in touch for a while but, I don't know, we're never home when he calls. He's been worried about us. All this time, it turns out. It just took him forever to get up the courage to try and get in touch. So, I told him about Mom and her situation and you'll never guess what he said. He said, 'Come on down and hang out in Mexico for a while. Let me see what I can do to buck you guys up.'"

He pulled a torn envelope out of the nook below the radio and held it face out to me and there was Dad's name and an address in Baja del Mar, Mexico.

"Where'd you get that?" I said.

"From the checks he sends Mom," said Will.

I studied the cut on his forehead. It looked pretty deep. I didn't want to know where or how he got it. I didn't want to know anything. I was all filled up with things I knew, and they just made me heavier, sadder, more heartbroken.

"Aren't you happy?" he said. "I thought this was what you wanted. We're going to see *Dad*! He wants to help us, just like you've always hoped he would!"

Happy? What I wanted?

I had no idea at that point what I wanted. Did I even know what happy looked like anymore? But what if Dad *had* called? Everything in me yearned to believe he had, and yet how could I? I mean, obviously, Dad hadn't called. Will was so amped up, I wouldn't have been surprised if he'd said we were being chased by purple elephants. But if Dad hadn't called, why were we headed down there? If that was where we were headed.

"Yeah," I said. "It's exciting."

And if it was true? If we really were going to see Dad? Would he help me? Was it too much to hope for that? It was all I had to cling to at that moment.

I shut my eyes—it was just too much, trying to get my head

around what was going on. I couldn't do it. Every time I got close, my thoughts would drift to the fact that I was trapped here, that I was Will's prisoner. I'd get a stab of panic and all the connections I'd been about to make would be erased just like that. I'd have to start all over.

Finally, I gave up. I tried to relax, to just pretend I wasn't there, that nothing was there, that I was disappearing along with the nightmare my life had become, and when I returned, my world would be back to normal. I somehow must have succeeded in falling asleep, because the next thing I knew, it was dark out and we were speeding down Highway 5, toward L.A. Will had the music going, softly, one of those instrumental metal bands he likes so much. I can't keep them straight, they all just sound like sci-fi music to me.

We were out in that part of central California where the land sort of sprawls out forever in all directions. Flat lines of darkness inside the night. No lights. No other cars. Nothing.

"Spooky, huh?" Will said.

"Yeah."

"It's like we're the only people alive on earth."

He was right. But to me, that was not a happy thought at all anymore.

WILL

We'd been driving through the void, just us and the Eagle and the darkness around us for hours, and it did things to me, sent me tumbling off into an alternate space that felt more like the world I wanted to live in than Morro Bay ever had. This was a place of emptiness, a place without people and their brutal selfish intentions. Just me and Asheley, safely encased in our bubble, foraging through the wilderness. I could have stayed on that road forever.

But a man's got to eat. And if I was going to make good on my promise to protect Ash, I had to make sure she ate too.

Sometime around eleven, we pulled into the In-N-Out on Highway 5. I would have wanted to stop off somewhere less conspicuous, but on that stretch of road, you've got no choice. It's that one In-N-Out or nothing.

The place was jam-packed. After hours of nothing, here was civilization in all its grotesqueness, these creatures who seemed to have crawled up out of the desert, salamanders and snakes and roaches and field mice taking human form, bloating themselves up and filling out their jeans and Bermuda shorts and their loud tacky surf wear until they approximated the obese ugly Americans you'd expect to find stuffing their faces at a fast food joint. It's like they'd all shown up just to get in our way.

I told Ash, "Be careful. You never know what kind of trouble these jokers might make for you."

"I will," she said. "Will, I'll be careful. I promise."

Just to be sure, I put an arm on her shoulder, walked her in like she belonged to me or something. I mean, looking at her, I had to do something. She'd changed out of that dumpy work uniform and was wearing her powder blue short-shorts—well, not that short, but short enough—and an aqua tank top that, cause she'd been sleeping in the car, was twisted all out of shape and hugging her breasts. She was ripe and adorable, her hair hanging droopy over her face like she needed someone to pull it behind her ear for her. She looked ready to be plucked. I knew I wasn't the only one who'd see it, so . . .

Anyway, she appreciated my chivalry. She leaned into me. She nuzzled.

People stared.

Check that. *Men* stared. They ogled. They drooled. The place pulsed with their desire for her as we walked in. There was an old guy in a Harley shirt with a handlebar mustache sitting at one of the tables near the door, and he almost jumped out of his seat and rushed up to manhandle Asheley right there.

And another guy, clean-cut, in chinos and a polo shirt, sitting in a booth with his teenaged son, who actually leaned in and started whispering and pointing, telling the kid, *hey, that's what I'm talking about—that's the kind of girl you can take for a ride.*

Every single guy in the entire place. I'm telling you. The whole bunch of them deserved to be lined up and shot.

Ash was oblivious. Tired and pouty. And that just made it worse. She had no idea what was going on. She thought these guys were all there just to chow down on burgers.

Even the bozos working the line were all over her, shooting each other these knowing looks, cracking dirty-minded smiles back and forth, trying to keep themselves from laughing. I swear, I almost leapt over the counter and popped them one.

I mean, what does it take to keep somebody safe? Can a girl not even walk into a fast food restaurant without everybody wanting to rape her?

The whole thing got me so mad I wasn't hungry anymore. I just wanted to beat the shit out of those fuckers.

It wasn't irrational. No way. You've seen her. You've met her. Don't tell me you haven't noticed her charms.

See, I can tell just from the smirk on your face that you understand what I'm talking about here, and . . .

You know what? Let me see her. What have you done to her? I swear to God, if I find out you've done something to her, I'll rip this whole fucking place apart! What happened to our deal?! I thought we had a deal?!

Trust you. Right. I can't trust anyone when it comes to Asheley. But you're right about that. I don't have any choice.

ASHELEY

Absolutely everything was setting him off. He couldn't keep still, kept glancing every which way to see who was staring at us and what they wanted, like he thought the whole world was going to gang rush us, pile on top of us and sink us to the ground, then pull out their knives and cut us to pieces.

It was like he'd lost his ability to differentiate between what was real and what wasn't. Everywhere he turned, he saw another villain itching to snatch me up as soon as he let his guard down.

And the thing is, I mean, really? Nobody was staring. We were at a fast food joint, just like any other fast food joint in the whole world. The bored kids working the cash registers and making the burgers. The tired parents with their whiney kids. Old people. Lonely old guys sitting like ghosts in the corners.

They could have cared less who we were and what we were up to. They all just wanted to get where they were going.

Try explaining that to him, though. It was almost impossible. The only way I could keep him from hyperventilating, from leaping over the booth and throwing punches, was to physically hold him still, like to place my hands over top of his and squeeze, to draw all that manic rage through them into me.

I said to him, "Will, Will, look at me. Don't look at these other people. They're nobody. They don't matter. All that matters is me. You and me. That's it. We're together, right Will? Remember? And as long as we're together, nobody can touch us. Wonder Twins, remember? Will, remember?"

And I kept his eyes locked in mine and pressed my hands into his until they stopped shaking.

"Okay, Will?" I said. "We're going to be fine. You're going to keep me safe until we get to Dad's house and then we'll be free. We'll start our lives all over."

What I saw in his face wasn't so much rage and hatred but fear. A deep fear beyond anything I'd ever seen in him before. It was like we were in the eye of a hurricane, and as long as I held him here, we'd be safe from harm, but if I let him stray, if I let him look outward toward the people outside our booth, he might swoop into a defensive swirl of activity, swinging and slashing, causing random destruction. It was my job to remain calm, and even though this was tough to do under the circumstances, I managed to get his breathing to slow down, to get him to eat his burger and reel himself back in, and somehow leave the restaurant and get back on the road.

It made me sad, really. So, so sad.

As we headed back onto the highway and continued racing south through the dark night, I wondered, where would he be, what would his life be like without me? Cause nobody, not one single person in the world, was able to reach him and rein him in except me.

How much worse would the things he'd done be if I weren't there?

I wondered, what would it take to fix him? Was it even possible?

I wished more than anything that he could one day somehow find some peace in his life. I still do. Maybe it's wrong of me, but I still do. Somewhere deep, deep inside him is a kind, sensitive person, and that's the Will I still see when I think of him. It's just, that Will's been so buried underneath this other one, who—it's like all the hurt in his life has made him into someone who only knows how to smash back at the world now.

There were no answers to these questions. They just made me sadder.

Meanwhile, I had to be as strong as I possibly could. Whether I was up to the task or not. I had to be steady, compassionate.

Get us to Mexico. Get us to Dad's house. That's what mattered.

Dad.

Another one of the memories I have of him came floating back to me as we rode southward. He used to throw me up above his head, probably not too high, just a few inches or so, but it felt a lot higher, like he was throwing me way, way up there. And the thing I remember most about him doing this is the feeling of flying way up there in the sky. I'd flap my arms. I'd feel like I was soaring. And then my stomach would leap as I headed back down. I used to beg him to do it. I couldn't get enough of it. Something about him raising me over his head, letting go, and then, most importantly, catching me again, it made me feel like, no matter how out of control my life got, he'd always be waiting down there to break my fall.

He loved us. And he'd help us. I knew he would. He'd been trying for years, in his way. I was sure of it. That's what kept me going through that ride down. Dad loved us and he'd know what to do to protect us.

WILL

We crossed the border around dawn the next morning. No problems. Or no problems with being searched or any of that. The guards gave us their usual power trip, throwing their condescending, suspicious smirks around, ogling Asheley as though they had any idea what kind of person she was, quizzing us on every last detail of where we'd come from and why we were so far from home. How old are you? Do your parents know where you are? What's up with the Deadhead sticker on your car? All that crap.

"Yes," I said. "Thank you very much. We're headed to Baja del Mar to see our dad."

"Baja del Mar. That's ritzy. What's your dad do?"

Asheley sat there smiling and looking cute. She let me do the talking, which was good. I can only imagine the trouble they'd have given her if she'd opened herself up to their teasing and flirting. They were already spending way too much time staring at her breasts and licking their lips. Like she was a piece of chicken or something.

"He's an architect. He's expecting us." As I held the envelope with Dad's address up for them to see, I gave them my best Obi-Wan Kenobi, a heavy, calm confidence, willing them toward the conclusion that we didn't have any droids on us.

It must have worked, because they waved us past and we were suddenly in Mexico. God that felt good. Like a whole new life had opened up to us, like the people we'd been had been left behind and now we could become anyone we wanted to be. It was thrilling.

Patting Asheley's knee, I said. "Here we go. Into the great unknown. You ready?"

She nodded. "You think he'll look like we remember him?" she asked.

"Who? Dad? A little grayer. A little tanner, probably, I guess. Who cares? We're in Mexico. Me-ki-ko!"

Wrong tactic. She sort of shrunk into herself at that. "I care, Will," she said. "I mean . . . You think he'll recognize us? Or we'll recognize him? It's . . . I'm nervous."

"Well, he called," I said. "He must want to see us. He said so explicitly. It's going to be awkward for the first little while, but then, you know? We'll catch him up on the people we've turned into and, you know? It'll be fine. We'll all be together. Really, Ash. Believe me." I felt terrible, lying to her like that, but not as bad as I felt seeing her face prune with worry and fear. "Regardless, we're in Mexico now! We're on an adventure! Let's get into the spirit!"

She raised her hands above her head and shook them around. She let loose a feeble "Yay!"

"All right, then," I said. "I'm driving. You're on navigation. You got the map?"

"Yes, master."

"Okay, then, away we go!"

It took us most of the day to get to Baja del Mar.

First we spent forever getting around the crush of traffic in Tijuana, all these rusty clunkers—that's what the Mexicans drove—and SUVs with American plates, full of young guys cruising for a nasty good time—all of them driving every which way, like they had no idea what the lines on the road were for, like the street lights weren't even there. That and the pedestrians—women in too-tight dresses and men wearing their shirts unbuttoned halfway to the waist, squinting out at the world from under their cowboy hats.

I couldn't help thinking that these people—every single one of them—were up to unsavory things. The women were all whores. The men were all out to debase and abuse them. Not a place for us to be. Not a place, anyway, for Asheley. Just thinking about what these guys wanted to do to her got me itching to take a knife to their throats.

But she kept me calm. She got us through and out to the coast road, where I was glad to see there wasn't much traffic at all. A truck full of dusty workingmen rolled by every once in a while. A bright Mexican family out strolling with their children, picking flowers along the side of the road, holding hands, dreaming their Mexican dreams.

We took our time.

We enjoyed ourselves.

We stopped along a sun-baked cliff to take in the view of the ocean, which was different down here—brighter, faded, less threatening. We stopped to get fish tacos and bottled water at an open-air restaurant painted in thick green and red stripes. Asheley convinced me to try the *horchata*, even though I suspected it might be contaminated. Once the coast dipped toward the water and the cliffs evened out, we stopped to run along the beach and get our feet wet in the surf.

It was nice. As long as there weren't any other people around, and Asheley was safe, and I was relaxed, we were fine—more than fine. We were at peace in a weird way. And, I mean, do you have any idea what that meant to us? I don't think I'd ever experienced peace before. It was an alien concept. Something I'd always figured was for other people, not me, never me. No way.

But for this one span of time, this one afternoon, as we drove south along the Mexican coastal road, there I was living the life I'd never thought I could have. Asheley and me both. It was maybe the most perfect my life's ever been. And thinking I could share this experience with Ash—I mean, I had to keep biting my lip to stop myself from tearing up.

All good things must end, though.

We rolled into Baja del Mar around seven that evening, and I mean, I don't know what I'd been expecting, but it wasn't this. The place reeked of money. I mean, you know, you live here, but I wasn't expecting all the houses hidden behind ornate fences and carefully pruned bougainvilleas lining the streets.

I found us a motel that looked like it might be within our

price range. Yeah, sort of low rent—or as low rent as motels get down here. Posada El Delfin, that's what it was called. You know it? Not a bad place. A little worn around the edges, some cracks in the whitewashed concrete.

I mean, the guy who works the desk is a dirtbag, but big surprise, right? I don't remember what his name was. Maybe Julio? Juan? Young guy, maybe twenty, twenty-one. And really skinny. Like, way, way too skinny. With these big hollow rat eyes.

While we were working out the deal for a room for the night, Ash told him explicitly, "Two beds." She motioned to me and said, "He's my brother." And what did the guy do? He winked at her and said, "*Si*, I understand." Then he did a mime of locking his lips shut with a key and checked us into a room with one queen size.

I'm sure he thought he was doing us a favor. He probably gets this kind of thing all the time, some couple—some whore with her "boyfriend," trying to look legit, or some old rich guy with his jailbait girlfriend claiming she's his daughter, or whatever, people can be disgusting in about ten thousand ways—winking and nodding their way through the check-in process, trying to ask for what they want without coming out and saying it, but still.

Do we look like those kinds of sleazeballs, though?

I guess it doesn't matter. We needed a room, and this is what the guy gave us. I can sort of understand the way he was thinking. Not that I like it, but I guess I get it. It's not like people expect to run into somebody as trusting and innocent as Asheley. There's, like, one of her for every thousand or so sluts out there. The whole thing left a bad taste in my mouth, though.

Even though we were completely legit, no bad intentions at all, I still ended up feeling dirty.

Anyway, we got our bags up into the room, which was nice—air conditioning and watercolors on the walls, all that—and we got ourselves situated a little bit.

We didn't really discuss what we'd do for the night, but my plan was for us to freshen up and then find somewhere to grab dinner. I figured, I mean, this town is fancy—I thought we might be able to find some incredible restaurant, like with an outdoor patio and candles in hurricane glasses on the table, maybe one of those places along the beach with a view of the sunset and the yachts docked off the coast, where we could celebrate with some *chiles rellenos* or mole or something. That was my hope, anyway.

While Ash gathered up her toothbrush and shampoo and all that and headed off to take a shower, I lay down on the bed and let myself relax. I'd been driving for two days straight. It had been even more than that since I'd slept.

I guess I nodded off.

I woke up to Ash nudging me on the shoulder.

"Will," she said. "Hey, you going to take a shower?"

One look at her, and my heart started breaking.

I mean, she was beautiful, and fragile, and just glowing with hope. It was precious, really. Heartbreaking. She'd made herself all up. She'd put on that Stanford sweatshirt. I'm not so stupid that I couldn't see what was bopping around in her mind.

"Yeah, I guess I will," I said, about the shower. "In a few minutes. You look like you're getting ready for something special."

This made her blush.

"Well," she said, "we're here. I thought we could head over to Dad's place tonight. I mean . . ."

"I know what you mean."

There was all this expectation roiling around on her face. If I could only begin to explain to you how sad it made me to see her like this.

Scooting over to the far side of the bed, I turned onto my side and patted the mattress in front of me. "Come," I said. "Sit."

She could sense I was about to deliver bad news. "What's wrong?" she said. "Will, don't look at me like that."

I tried to smile, to put her at ease, but it was hard. I was so, so, so sad for her.

"Just, come."

Timidly, she did. She scooched up onto the bed and sat next to where I was lying. Waited there, silent and nervous, for what I was about to say.

"How much do you remember about Dad?" I said.

"I don't know. A lot."

"Like what?"

"I remember how he used to sit in the living room with his legs crossed, bouncing me up and down on his foot, playing horsey, and he'd ask me silly questions about my day."

"What else?"

"I remember him building that jungle gym we used to have in the backyard. I don't know. Why does it matter, Will?"

I sat up. I took her hands in mine and held them. The air conditioning was going full blast and I suddenly realized how cold the room was.

"It's just . . . I just . . . Ash, those are both things you've seen in pictures of him. Do you remember anything about who he was? I mean for real, not just smiling for the camera?"

"I don't know. I mean, yeah. Let me think."

"You don't, Ash. You don't. 'Cause if you did, you'd know, Dad's a . . . he's a bad guy. He's not any of those nice things you remember him being. You wonder why Mom drinks the way she does? You wonder why she works so hard to destroy herself? It's cause of Dad. She's chasing away her memories of Dad. I'm sorry, Ash. I'm—"

"Why are you telling me these things right now?" she said.

I could feel the muscles in her hands tensing up, and I massaged her knuckles a tiny bit trying to calm her down.

"He's not going to help us," I said. There it was, the brutal truth. I wish there'd been some way for me not to say it, but I'd run out of time. She had to know. "Come," I said. "Come."

I tugged at her hand, lightly, and she let me place her on the bed in front of me so I could massage her shoulders.

"I'm sorry. I can't tell you how sorry I am," I said.

"It's okay," she whispered. She was holding it all in, all the shock and sadness she must have been feeling in that moment. I was proud of her. She was being very brave.

"But, hey," I said. "We're in Mexico. Far, far away from Morro Bay. That's the good thing. And we've got each other." I wrapped my arms around her waist and hugged her. "What else do we need?"

I let my hand go up under her sweatshirt and opened my palm flat on her soft abdomen. It's something I'd been longing to do since forever.

"Wonder Twins, right?" I said.

Then I kissed her on the tender spot where her neck meets her collarbone and squeezed her tight and held her, rocking her a little.

"Yeah," she said. "Wonder Twins."

She patted my knee, and almost daintily, unwrapped my arms from around her. Standing up she said, "I saw a Coke machine out by the office. One of those old kinds, with the bottles. I'm going to go get one. I'm dying of thirst."

As she walked past me, she squeezed my shoulder.

And then she was gone.

ASHELEY

There were reasons to hope. Will had come through in a kind of way. At least, he'd brought me to the place he'd told me we were going. And Dad *did* live here. I knew that for fact. Will and I hadn't worked out when we were going to head over to his house, but I'd waited so long, there's no way I was going to wait another day. The tricky part would be to convince Will to go along with it.

Instead of trying to solve that problem, I concentrated on the good stuff. Dad. He was so close I could almost hear him calling out my name. All these stupid, childlike questions raced through my head. Would he look the same? Would he still smell the way I remembered? Would he like me? Would he understand my insecurities and fears without my having to say them out loud, or would I have to spell every little thing out for him, tell him exactly how frightened I was, of Will, of the future, of absolutely everything? I felt sort of like I was about to go on a blind date and I didn't want to blow it.

After my shower, I got myself all made up, eyeliner, mascara, blush, the works. Not trashy, just . . . I wanted to look nice for him. I patted a little bit of perfume on my wrists and everything.

Then I put on my favorite pair of jeans and the Stanford sweatshirt I love so much. Maybe he'd make the connection and realize that I was wearing it for him. Like he'd see it and he'd know I'd kept loving him all this time, and forgiven him, whatever his reasons might have been, for running away from us all those years ago.

My hair still wet, I returned to the room.

Will was snoring there, sprawled out across the crisp made bed in the clothes he'd been wearing for two days. He hadn't even taken his shoes off. I let him sleep—he was less scary that way—and rooted through my bag for a pair of clean socks.

The sun had begun to set while I was in the shower, and the angle of the window, combined with the fading light, made for a lot of shadows and darkness in the room. I turned on a couple lights so it wouldn't be so gloomy.

Shoes tied and ready to go, I shook him awake.

"Will," I said. "Hey, you going to take a shower?"

"Yeah, I guess I will," he said. "In a few minutes."

He stretched. He luxuriated in the size of the bed, smiling up at me like all his cares had been left far away in California, like he'd reached his destination. No urgency at all. And none of the panic and paranoia and twitchiness that had been so constant over the past few days.

He looked me up and down through heavy-lidded eyes. This is not right, I thought. He's way too content. The calm before the storm, I thought. And I felt a tug that said, *Go, find Dad, now before it's too late.*

"You look like you're getting ready for something special," he said.

"I am getting ready for something special," I said. "Go take your shower. If you're quick enough, we could head over tonight, don't you think?" I was trying to keep my pep up, to infect him with my positivity.

He sat up at this and made a disconcerted face. "Come," he said. "Sit."

It was like he had a secret, some sick thing he was thinking, and it was spilling out through his bloodshot eyes. The twitchiness was returning, too, mostly in the tips of his fingers.

"What's wrong?" I said. "Will, don't look at me like that."

"Just, come."

Best not to upset him, was what I was thinking. I sat next to him on the bed.

"What's up?" I said. "Will, this seems like a game and I'm not really in the mood for it."

That's when he launched into this long diatribe, accusing Dad of everything from beating Mom senseless every night, to sleeping with every woman in the Bay area. "He's the most selfish person I've ever met," he said. "You don't know. You were too young to remember. But I can tell you, all those things you've imagined him to be, he's the opposite of that. Think of Satan, and then multiply by ten."

Eventually I couldn't take it anymore. I wanted to scream at him, tell him to take a look at himself, for once. "Why are you telling me these things right now?" I said, keeping as calm as I could.

He took my hands then, and started massaging my fingers.

"Because, you should know, he's not going to help us," he said.

I didn't know whether to believe him or not. I didn't want to believe him. He had all kinds of reasons to be lying to me. But in his sick way, he loved me, so maybe, I don't know, maybe he thought he was being noble and kind somehow.

"Come," he said again. "Come." Like his only concern was my shattered emotions and his hopes of calming them, comforting me. And he pulled me by the arms toward himself.

I didn't have much choice. I let myself be maneuvered in front of him so I was sitting with my back nestled up against his chest and I let him wrap his arms around my waist.

"I'm sorry," he said. "I can't tell you how sorry I am."

But I wasn't listening anymore. I was paying attention to what he was doing with his hands, snaking them under my sweatshirt, flicking them across my skin, probing in a way, way too directed manner for any of this to be accidental.

"It's okay," I murmured, more to me than to him.

"But, hey," he said. "We're in Mexico. Far, far away from Morro Bay. That's the good thing. And we've got each other. What else do we need?"

When his hand began inching up my stomach toward

my bra line, I reached up and held it still. He spun me slowly around so I was facing him and he steadied me with his hands on my hipbones.

The look on his face! It told me everything. It filled me with revulsion. He thought this was some sort of honeymoon for us and that we were going to melt together now. How could he have thought that, though? Had I led him on? I couldn't stop thinking that this was all my doing, even though I'd never once—not once—treated him like anything more than my brother. Yeah, we'd cuddled a few times earlier in the summer— chastely, just holding each other in fear, basically—but, I don't know, I had this sense that I'd misunderstood his feelings . . . that I'd been thinking all along that he was trying to protect me like any brother would when actually he had other ideas entirely.

I was nauseous. Seriously. I came about *this* close to throwing up.

And what would he do to me if I said no to him?

He nuzzled his face into my chest.

He started kissing me.

"Wonder Twins, right?" he whispered in my ear.

"Yeah," I said. "Wonder Twins." But everything inside me was shouting, *No, no no! I'm not your Wonder Twin, not if this is what you meant by the phrase!*

He'd gotten it all wrong. The thought of a sexual relationship with him was so sickening to me that it made me want to turn my body inside out, to leave my body and its curves behind forever, go whispering away to a place where my body didn't exist, where nobody would ever desire it again.

But it wasn't that easy.

He was kissing me on the lips now. He was using his tongue!

I was terrified. I had to get away from him. As fast and far away as I could. The only safe choice I had in that moment, though, was to resist as subtly as I possibly could and endure until I found a way to get him to let me go. I'm pretty good at psychologically arming myself—I've been doing it for years in order to deal with Mom. But if Will turned violent—which I was afraid he might if I disobeyed him—if he physically restrained me from leaving the room, I had no defense against that. He's way, way stronger than I am. I had to be careful, keep him thinking that I had infinite trust in him.

My arms still wrapped around him, I gazed deep into his eyes, hoping that instead of my fear, he'd see the expression on my face as lusty. I ran my finger along his scruffy face. "I desperately need something to drink," I said. "I saw a Coke machine out by the office. One of those old kinds, with the bottles. I'm going to go get one. Then I'll be right back. Okay?"

And oh my God, it worked. He released me.

I patted his knee reassuringly.

"I'll be right back," I said again. "Promise."

And somehow I managed not to start running until the door was shut tight behind me.

WILL

It took me ten minutes to start getting worried.

I kept thinking about the smirk the guy at the front desk had given me as he handed over our key. He'd practically pissed himself when he'd seen Asheley, like jaw dropping, eyes bulging, drooling, the whole works. What wouldn't he do to get his hands on her? My guess was there wasn't much. He figured she was just an American whore, and who'd notice or care if he carted her away and used and abused her, then dumped her body along the side of the road when he was done. Happens all the time. These guys think women exist for their own pleasure. You could see it in his face—those dark hollow eyes, that crooked mouth and rat nose—he wasn't above anything to get what he wanted.

And Asheley out there all alone. Stupid. So stupid.

And me still lying there on the hotel bed, waiting around for the inevitable tragedy to occur. Jesus.

I leapt up. I raced out the door into the dry hot air and looked around. A wide-open parking lot, a dumpster in the corner. Those low, whitewashed concrete walls that line every street in town. Now that it was getting dark out, there was something ghostly to the place. Like all of a sudden the dead were up walking around with the living.

No sign of Asheley and the rat boy, though. Fuck.

I was more angry at myself than her. It wasn't her fault everybody found her sexy. She was born that way. But me, I was aware of the situation and so I should have tagged along to ward the bastards off.

In a far dark corner of the parking lot, a group of four guys were passing a bottle around. Mexican guys. Squat and round, wearing faded guayabera shirts that looked like they might be as old as the guys were.

"Hey!" I shouted, stomping toward them, peacocking, pointing at them, so they knew I meant business. "Where'd they go?"

"Where'd who go?"

One guy did all the talking. The others just hung back, snickering to each other.

"You know who. The girl. The fucking desk clerk."

"I don't know. We just got here, man."

I was on top of them now, hulking over them, stepping in too close, letting them know I wasn't afraid of anything they had and they better deal with me or there'd be consequences.

"Bullshit you just got here. You want to get into it? I can get into it if that's how you're gonna be," I said. I took a step forward, puffed out my chest. I grabbed the bottle away from him and waved it around like a weapon.

"I'm serious, man. Go ask the guy at the desk if you don't believe me." He pointed at the office.

Through the plate glass window, I could just see the top of the clerk's head above the check-in desk. He was still there. I raced toward him.

"Hey, man, give us our tequila back, hey?"

I stopped. And I looked at them. And I don't know why, maybe just cause I felt like it, cause I was surging with aggression and rage, I reared back and threw the bottle as far as I could toward the buildings and streets out past the cement wall. The guys ducked like I'd just thrown a bomb, kept their heads down, waiting for the sound of shattered glass in the distance. Then they stood back up and started shouting at me in Spanish.

"Gringo asshole," they said. "You owe us another bottle of tequila."

But I didn't care. I was already yanking the door to the office off its hinges. Storming in and pounding my hands on the counter.

"What'd you do with her?" I said. "Give me my sister right now, motherfucker, or I swear, I'll tear you into a million pieces."

The guy had been watching soccer—I know, I know, "football," whatever—the guy had been watching soccer on a beat-up old TV mounted in the corner of the room, and he took his smart-ass time getting around to looking at me. And then he just stared—he didn't say a word. He had a bag of tortilla chips open in front of him, and a mess of crumbs all over the desk. And every few seconds, he'd pull another chip out and chomp down on it, making a loud crunch.

"Problem?" he said.

"My sister. What the fuck did you do with her?"

"Your sister? You mean that girl I saw go running past half an hour ago? Man, I'll tell you what, she was crying, man. What did you do to her?" Really. That's what he said. Then he crunched into another chip and shrugged. "Sorry, man," he said. "Can't help you there. I don't get involved in domestic disputes."

And that was it. He went back to staring at his soccer game.

So, why didn't I lunge across the desk and smack him up? Good question. I don't know. He didn't have Asheley. So fuck him, I left. I hopped in the Eagle and peeled out of the parking lot, figuring the town's not that big, I could drive up and down every single street and I'd have to find something, right? Asheley's sweatshirt or a shoe or something. And when I did, then . . . motherfuckers better watch out.

Up and down and up and down, from the foothills to the beach back to the foothills to the beach. And I didn't see another living soul. It was like the whole town knew what had happened to Asheley and it terrified them and they'd all locked themselves in their houses for the night. Like the night was for the ghosts and the gangs and the fools willing and stupid enough to challenge them.

For the next, like, five hours, I drove like a madman all over town and I couldn't find her anywhere. I'd probably still be driving around, but at some point, as my thoughts bounced through the possible scenarios, I realized: Dad.

I checked the slot on the dash where I'd stuffed the address. It was missing.

And I knew what had happened, it was all suddenly clear. She so idealized him. The asshole. You know, there was one day, right near the end, like a month before he disappeared from our lives for good. It was already obvious that he and Mom hated each other, that all they'd ever do was make each other's lives hell. I'd been out on a playdate. Hanging around at one of my little friends' houses, and he'd been supposed to come pick me up. I can't remember all the specifics, who the friend was, why I'd been over at his house, but I do remember that for some reason his family was going out that afternoon. Some important thing, I don't know. And there was a kind of a tight window during which Dad needed to come get me. And he didn't come. We called and everything, and nobody picked up. And eventually my friend's family told me they couldn't wait any longer and they locked me out of the house, left me there to wait. And wait. And wait. And it got to be, like, three hours and I was still waiting there, sitting on the lip of their front stoop. And . . . I ended up eventually walking the whole way home. Like ten miles. And when I got there, Dad was out in the front lawn practicing his putting, just totally oblivious to what he'd done to me. And this is the part that's stayed with me most vividly. He grinned at me. He winked. "Hey little man," he said. "Where've you been?" He'd totally forgotten. That's how important I was to him. I burst into tears, bawling uncontrollably. Feeling the void, the absolute emptiness of the world around me. Terrified. Sure that the world would gobble me up. And nobody would care. When I pulled it together to speak, I said, "Dad, I was waiting for you. Why didn't you come pick me up like you said you would?" He bent down on a knee to meet me eye to eye and said, "Is that what I said?" I nodded. "Well, I guess that's a lesson to you, huh? You found your way home. You don't need me." But I did. I did need him. The real lesson was that he didn't care. And what would happen when Asheley realized this too? She'd shatter. She'd crumble. She'd be ruined by him. All the things I'd spent my whole life trying to protect her from.

I headed toward his address. One Ensenada Road. I trolled my way there slowly, hoping against hope that I'd see Ash stumbling down the street along the way and be able to pick her up, and maybe, I don't know, convince her of what a bad idea this was.

My big worry at that point was that she might have beat me there, that she might have to confront him all by herself.

It must have been two or three in the morning by the time I arrived. Dad's house was warded off, away from the street, not by one of those low cement walls that were everywhere, but by a much bigger wall, white stones carefully bonded in place, tapered pillars every six or eight feet. Through the wrought iron gate blocking off the driveway, I could see the estate. It was huge. Like, acres of land spanning all the way to what must have been a private beach, and the ocean. The house itself was almost identical to ours, the same rounded walls, the same multilevel sections, the same off-kilter windows, everything. Dad's style, it turns out, hadn't changed all that much. But where ours was a dark woody brown, this one was a pinkish, yellowish white, the color of scallop shells, or that's what I gathered from what I could make out. It was pretty dark out there. The lights were all out. Dad and whoever else he might have in that house were asleep.

So I sat at the corner of the driveway and leaned against the wall and waited. Asheley would find her way here eventually. And then, she'd see for herself how much love Dad had to throw her way. What would happen then? Who would she have left?

Me, that's who. Me and only me.

This was my last chance to stop her. To save her. And if I failed? I knew what would happen then. Game over. We'd end up in the hands of you guys. And she didn't deserve that. I've said a thousand times, none of this is her fault.

ASHELEY

I ran and I ran, until I couldn't run anymore, then I walked, for hours, it seemed like, along the beach, along these dark residential streets packed with tiny Spanish-style houses with ceramic roofs that looked like they were made of glued-together shards of broken pottery, along stretches of garden dense with floral scents, all these shadows and nooks and crannies where who knows what might have been hiding, Will, or who knows, some other dangerous guy—every shift in the wind, every fluttering of the leaves, made me jump—and then the big houses started up, the villas and mansions and then, my God, there it was: Ensenada Road.

The tears came crashing back—tears of relief this time—and I didn't try to stop them. I was seeing myself ringing the doorbell to Dad's house, seeing his face peer out the window for a moment, checking to see who it was, and then, when he recognized me, opening into a smile. He'd throw open the door. He'd gather me into his great arms and hold me tight and safe. It was about to happen. It was moments away.

I wandered down the road, checking the numbers on the houses. It was pitch-black outside, total darkness. The moon had set hours earlier.

I was nervous. I was starting to get a little squirrelly with hope.

And that's when I saw the Eagle parked haphazardly across both lanes of traffic, the door still open, and the interior light faintly glowing inside.

But disturbingly, no Will.

I seized up with terror. For all I knew, he was watching me right that minute, planning some ambush. I'd betrayed him. He must have realized this by now. And he's not the type of guy to forgive people who've betrayed him.

I crept low to the ground, clinging to the shadows along the high stone wall that lined the road, slipping from entryway to entryway like a soldier trying to avoid sniper fire.

Every minute or so, I'd pause and listen for a footstep, a breath, some sign of Will's location. But there was no sound, just the waves in the distance.

Slowly, slowly, I inched up toward the Eagle.

Something moved in the shadows, at the edge of my vision, and I jumped. I let out a yelp. A lizard. Just a lizard. But for a moment there, I couldn't even breathe.

I crept forward. The Eagle was right in front of me now—two more driveway nooks to go, then I'd be there. I bent to the ground to see if Will was lurking on the other side, but nothing. Nothing I could see.

Maybe I was wrong. Maybe Will had fallen asleep in the back of the Eagle, was hunkered down in there hidden from my view. There weren't any bushes for him to hide behind, just the stone pillars that marked off the driveways.

I stood up. I relaxed just the slightest bit, thinking I knew where he might be and where he might not, thinking Dad's house must be right up ahead here, and the best thing to do now was get quickly to it.

Speed-walking, I darted past the Eagle, glanced inside—no Will sleeping there—and slipped around the pillar of the next driveway. This one was closed off by a heavy whitewashed iron gate, and I didn't even have to look at the number to know that this was absolutely Dad's house. It was uncanny how much it looked like our house—like our house transported off to paradise.

And suddenly, Will had my arms locked behind my back, one hand clamped over my mouth to muffle my scream. I bit his fingers. I kicked at his knees with the heel of my foot. Spinning and lurching, trying to throw him off of me.

"Ash," he was saying, his lips right up to my ear. "Ash, why did you run? You need to trust me. No one else can help you."

It was no use. He was stronger than me. I went limp.

Yeah, I mean, right at that moment, I had no idea what he would do. I thought he might try to . . . this is hard to, you know? To think of my brother in this way . . . sexually assault me, is what I'm trying to say. Like he had in the hotel room. Or he might try to kill me. If he thought I'd turned on him, I was afraid maybe he'd break my neck, leave me there to die, and . . .

WILL

No, of course not. No way would I have hurt her. I was there to protect her.

This whole thing—all of it—I didn't care what happened to me. I'm scum. I deserve whatever I've got coming. The whole point was to keep Asheley from being hurt.

I loved her.

Don't you understand that? I didn't matter. The only thing that mattered to me was her.

ASHELEY

The more I twisted and turned in his grip, the harder he squeezed my arms tight behind me. He kept whispering in my ear, "Don't do this, Ash. Just, please, don't do this. Remember? Wonder Twins? We don't need Dad to save us. We can save ourselves. The rest of them, Dad, everybody else out there, they'll tear us apart."

He was right. But he was wrong too. We couldn't save ourselves. The only way either of us would be saved was if someone—Dad—interceded and pried us away from each other.

My arms were twisted so tightly behind me. I don't think he realized his own strength.

"You're hurting me, Will," I said, and he let up a tiny bit, just enough for me to yank one arm away. I took the opportunity while I had it, lunged for the buzzer built into the wall, and jabbed at it with all my strength, praying that Dad would forgive me, once he heard my story, for sounding the alarm at this time in the morning.

And then something totally surprising happened. I couldn't believe it. Will let me go.

There were tears in his eyes. He was pleading with me. "Ash, no," he said, "Really. You don't want to see him." But he wasn't doing anything to stop me anymore.

"I do, Will. I have to," I said to him.

And something changed in him. The hope inside him went dead. It was weird. I could see it. His heart was breaking, and his body sagged a little on his bones. His eyes lost their fight. He slumped down and leaned back against the pillar. I'd just hurt him so bad. It was horrible.

But being here. Seeing Dad. I'd longed for this moment my entire life.

A lamp came on in the window way up at the top of the house, where Mom's room would have been in our house.

Another light came on, this one on the ground floor.

Then nothing.

My heart surging, I waited and waited and waited.

I rang the bell again. I couldn't stop myself. And a light came booming on from above my head. The intercom crackled. "Who's there?"

"Daddy, it's me. It's Asheley," I said. "I made it. I'm with Will . . ." But I don't think he heard me. The intercom had gone silent. Nobody responded.

I waited some more.

I wondered for a moment if I had the wrong house.

Some more lights came on inside the house. Isolated windows, lighting up then going dark again.

Finally, finally, the front door opened a crack and a silver-haired man in a plush bathrobe stepped outside. He was bigger than I'd expected. Taller. And broader. He had the wide chest of someone who'd luxuriated in success for many, many years, and a graying beard that he'd let grow wispy down around his neck. As he walked toward us, though, I knew—I just knew—it was Dad. It was there in his eyes. In the arc of his eyebrows and the slope of his earlobes. I'd studied my photos of him for so long I think I could have recognized him from his fingernails.

My lower lip started quivering. I had to keep telling myself not to cry.

When he got to the gate, he tightened the belt on his robe, and held himself up against one of the iron rods with a stiff arm. He didn't say a word. He just stared at me. There was action behind his eyes, cognition, a glimmer of recognition, but his face betrayed nothing. There was no emotion seeping out of him.

I was breaking down, though, so overwhelmed with emotion that I almost couldn't speak. The few words I managed to get out seemed so small, so useless compared to what was going on inside me.

"Daddy," I said. "Dad, it's us. We came. You called us, and we came right away."

I was four years old again. It was like my life had been frozen in time since the day he had left, and now finally I could live again.

He ticked his finger against the pole he was leaning on. I

noticed there was a gold chain hanging around his neck and I wondered who'd given it to him and what it symbolized. What was the size and shape of his life now?

"I'm not sure I understand what you mean," he said.

"On Sunday, when you called us, we came, right away," I said. "It's me. It's Asheley. And this is Will."

I nudged Will with my toe, and glanced down at him sitting there, watching intently, muttering silently to himself.

"I never called you people," Dad said.

Will stood up. He placed a hand on my shoulder, just resting it there, not tight.

"Well, we came anyway," I said. "We . . . I needed you. Daddy, I . . . I've been wanting to meet you my entire life." Will's hand pulsed on my shoulder, tightening slightly. I wasn't understanding yet what was going on. Or I wasn't willing to understand. I thought, somehow, if I explained myself clearly enough, Dad was still going to open the gate and let me in. Even though the look in his eyes had hardened. Even though I saw little heads behind him, two of them, children with long straight black hair, peering around the corner of the open door. They were just about the same ages Will and I had been when he'd left us behind way up there in California.

One of them asked him a question in halting Spanish and he turned and waved them back inside the house.

"Nobody," he answered, in English.

"Why are they here in the middle of the night?" the child asked.

"I don't know," he said. "Go back inside. Let's not wake up your mother."

That's when it sunk in. That's when I lost it. He'd left Will and me behind over a decade ago and he had no intention of letting us back in to his home, to his heart, to his life in any way. He didn't want us. Not Will. Not me.

"It's four thirty in the morning," he said. "You're disturbing my family. I'd like it if you people got in your car and headed back to wherever you came from."

I went a little crazy then. I guess, yeah, I overreacted. I threw myself into the gate. Pounded at it with my fists. Crying and screaming, "Let me in, Dad! Let me in! You know where we came from! You know! You know! We came from where you came from! Let me in! Dad! Dad! Please!" until I couldn't shout anymore. I was just all sobs and spasms.

The only thing keeping me from falling to the ground was Will holding me up, trying to calm me down.

And Dad just stood there, watching me. I thought, he must think I look pathetically stupid in my Stanford sweatshirt, so embarrassingly obvious in my love for him.

"Stop it, Ash. Stop it. Let it go," Will said. He held me tighter, wrapped his arms around me. Like he thought he could comfort me. As if that were possible.

"Daddy," I said. "Please. Do one thing for me. Only one. And then I swear, I'll never bother you again. You can forget I exist."

"I'm listening," he said, so quietly I almost couldn't hear him.

That's when I realized he was crying too. He was trying to hold it in, but I could tell. Tears were welling in his eyes.

I reached my arm through the gate and held my hand out to

him. Just to touch him. To feel close to him, just for a moment. And he let me do it. He held my hand in his. He acknowledged me. He said my name out loud. "Asheley." And Will's, too. I mean, Will hung back, he refused to get too close, but Dad looked at him and said, "Will. My little man."

He seized up then—the tears choked off his words—and he shook his head a few times trying to knock the tears away. "I messed it all up with you guys, didn't I?"

We didn't answer. Neither of us. I think we were too overwhelmed. Confused. Sad and happy, both. Not just me, Will too.

"I wish . . . I don't know what I wish," Dad said.

His tears came surging back, and he just stared at us, his eyes so glassy and wet that he must not have been able to see anything.

It was like he was begging us to release him.

"Just please, Daddy, please, we need help," I said. "We need the police. We need you to call them."

Dad pondered this request for a moment. Then he bowed his head and walked slowly back up the driveway. When he got to the front door, he looked back at us. I think he nodded. It was hard to tell. He brought a finger to his lips, like he was kissing us goodbye, saying a little prayer for our safe passage.

I couldn't process at all what had just happened. What I was was tired. So, so, so tired. I slid down the gate and let myself relax onto the blacktop at the lip of the driveway.

"They've got something called extradition, Asheley," Will said. "You know what that means? That means they'll send us home. We'll be arrested. We'll be . . . they won't let us be together anymore. Is that what you want?"

"I don't know, Will. I don't know what I want. I just want this crazy thing we're doing to stop."

Neither of us said anything for a while. Then he touched me on the shoulder.

"What are we going to do?" he said.

"You can do whatever," I said. "I'm going to sit here and wait for the cops."

He thought about this for a second or two. "I guess I will too, then," he said finally, plopping himself down next to me.

So, that's what we did. We sat there and waited for you guys to show up and you know what happened to us after that.

WILL

No, that's it. That's all of it.

You understand, though, right? I'm not some bloodthirsty psychopath. I wish I'd known some other way to go about it. To keep Ash safe.

But I didn't . . .

And she needed . . .

I had to do something.

So . . . yeah, do whatever it is you're going to do to me. I understand. I really could care less what happens to me. Just . . . our deal. Asheley. She's going to be okay, right? You'll go easy on her? She deserves a lot better than what I've put her through.

ASHELEY

I'm not saying I'm entirely innocent. If that were true, I wouldn't feel so horrible about all the little compromises I've made. What I'm saying is, he's my brother, you know? I love him. Even when he's wrong. Even when he's totally out of his head. I understand him. He needed me. He still needs me, I'm sure.

And I let him down.

I let everybody down. Him, Craig, Naomi, Keith.

And it's too late to change what happened, or to say sorry to any of them. I know that. I just wish . . .

You know what I keep thinking about? That day, playing softball and circling the bases, coming home safe. Everybody cheering and clapping me on the back. It was all so simple. I'd done something good and they appreciated me for it.

I want to have that feeling again sometime in my life. If I can earn it. I want to earn it. I want to know I can do something good. And I promise, I swear, if things work out after they transport me back to Morro Bay, I'm going to try to get past all this. I owe myself that much. And I owe it to Will. I mean, he's sort of a victim in all this too—can I stand up? I'm going to stand up now, okay?—I relied a little too much on his love for me. I wish more than anything that I could go back to that party we threw, that moment when Craig called and I dragged Will outside with me to go find him—I mean, no. I mean, that's not what I mean. I—